ALL OR NOTHING

SAFE IN LOVE
BOOK 2

TILYA ELOFF

CONTENTS

Content Warning	v
Playlist	vi
1. Jack	1
2. Jack	12
3. Harley	20
4. Harley	32
5. Jack	40
6. Harley	55
7. Jack	67
8. Harley	80
9. Jack	94
10. Harley	104
11. Jack	114
12. Harley	125
13. Jack	136
14. Harley	144
15. Jack	155
16. Harley	164
17. Jack	175
18. Harley	187
19. Jack	196
20. Harley	205
21. Jack	215
Epilogue	226
Other Books by Tilya	233
Where you can find me	234
Acknowledgments	235
About author	236
Note from the author	237

ALL or NOTHING

SAFE IN LOVE BOOK TWO

TILYA ELOFF

COPYRIGHT

Copyright © 2022 Tilya Eloff.
ALL OR NOTHING
SAFE IN LOVE BOOK TWO
Cover Designer and formatter: Liberty Parker

All rights reserved. No part of this publication may be reproduced, distributed, or transmitted in any form or by any means, including photocopying, recording, or other electronic or mechanical methods, without the prior written permission of the publisher, except in the case of brief quotations embodied in critical reviews and certain other noncommercial uses permitted by copyright law.

Any references to historical events, real people, or real places are used fictitiously. Names, characters, and places are products of the author's imagination.

CONTENT WARNING

Content warning: Graphic/mature language and actions, mentions of miscarriage, attempted sexual assault, child abandonment, and neglect. Reader's discretion advised.

PLAYLIST

Not Another Song About Love by Hollywood Ending
You Make Me Sick by P!nk
Ride 4 Me by Austin Tolliver
IDFC by Blackbear
Shivers by Ed Sheeran
34+35 by Ariana Grande
All or Nothing by Theory of a Dead Man
Bubbly by Colbie Caillat
Little Do You Know by Alex & Sierra
Mercy by Shawn Mendes
Cooler Than Me by Mike Posner & Gigamesh
Falling by Trevor Daniel
Crazy by K-Ci & JoJo
I Don't Want to Live Forever by Taylor Swift and Zayn Malik

I Think I'm In Love by Kat Dahlia
Him and I by G-Eazy and Halsey
Die A Happy Man by Thomas Rhett

Chapter 1

JACK

Christmas was eventful this year. Not only has Xander settled down with an exceptional woman who has two amazing kids. They also announced their pregnancy and got engaged all before lunch today. Things are bound to be different around here now, no more late guys' nights getting plastered. I guess that's not so terrible. We are getting too old for that shit, anyway. Well, that's not entirely true either, because that is precisely what Justin and I are doing tonight. It's not the same though, Xander and I have been through a lot together. Xander and I met during my freshman year of high school. I was in my fifth foster home, sour to the world and nothing but trouble, until Xander and his folks took me in. It was when his family took me in that I felt like I belonged somewhere. We were all devastated when his mom passed away only three days after Christmas that first year, I was with them. It was equally devastating when Ashley, Xander's sister, was killed by her abusive boyfriend. Xander and Pops had enough on their plate to deal with the passing of Mom, then on top of that Ashley had been killed our junior year. It was one helluva shit storm, and I was surprised that they were able to keep going. I missed them both like hell, but that was their blood, their family. I know they feel that way about me too, and I mourned right along with them when we lost Mom and Ashley. From then on, it was just Xander, Pops, and me. Now our little family is growing. Justin and I met while he and his crew were finishing up Xander's house. Since he skipped out on Christmas with the family, we're sitting around watching Die Hard, the best Christmas movie ever.

"So, you mean to tell me, I not only missed out on the announcement that my favorite cousin is expecting again but also missed her getting engaged and the bitch wasn't even there?" He grumbles for the second time as he takes a drag from the joint. I just passed him. Inhaling deeply, he passes it back to me, shaking his head. The bitch he is referring to is Becky, his ex-girlfriend. She's not a bitch, she is actually a really sweet girl, well, woman. When they broke up, they didn't end on the best of terms. No one really knows what happened and neither of them is sharing that piece of information. All of us wonder what happened though, to make those two go from being head over heels in love to fucking hating each other.

"That figures, she's always fucking up something in my life. It's like she takes great pleasure in it." Justin keeps mumbling as

I inhale deeply, enjoying the sticky smoke filling my lungs and losing up all my muscles.

"I highly doubt she skipped out on Christmas with them just to spite you, man. I'm sure she was just with her family. Did you even ask if she was gonna be there before you decided not to go?" I ask with a raised brow but already know the answer. He didn't, and he is pissed off for no reason. Instead, he chooses to ignore my question. He holds his hand out for me to pass the joint back to him.

"You wanna talk about what's really bothering you?" I ask, leaning my head back on the sofa.

"Nothing's bothering me. It's all in the past and doesn't mean dick now." He replies, but doesn't quite sound like he means it. I let it drop, knowing he isn't going to talk about it. Maddie has already tried with him and Becky. Neither of them will say a word about what happened between the two of them and until they do, it will keep making the rest of us extremely uncomfortable. None of us want to take sides, but we also want to be there for our friends. Trouble is, they are both our friends and none of us wants to get in the middle of that fucking circus. I decide to change the subject, not wanting to lose my buzz just yet.

"Hey man, you want a beer?" I ask as I get to my feet heading to the kitchen.

"Sounds good, man." He replies to my retreating back. In just a few brief steps, I reach the fridge, grab us both a beer, and the bag of chips off the counter. I head back to the living room.

My place isn't big. I live in a three-bedroom single-wide on three acres of land. It's all I could afford after moving back from New Orleans. Xander and I lived there for a couple of years after Xander got out of the military. We moved back recently and opened a tattoo parlor together. Even though it is only a single-wide trailer, it's more than I ever had growing up. No one can take from me. It's mine. Although if it weren't for the little bit of money my aunt left me, I would have never been able to afford this either. I never met my aunt and haven't ever heard from her. She had the money delivered to me after my dad, whom I also never met, passed away. Without that money, I would be still making payments instead of saving to build a house here. That is the end goal, build the perfect house on my little plot of land. Something I can be proud of.

My dad apparently cared enough to leave me a little money after he died but didn't care enough to have anything to do with me when he could when it mattered most. The letter said something to the effect of,

'I'm sorry I was never around, but my wife could never know about you, or she would have left and taken my kids with her, and they were the most important things in my life. Turns out that after finding out I have cancer; she left any way informing me they were never mine. I should have reached out to you earlier, but... well, I didn't know what to say. Maybe one day this letter will find its way to you.'

I may have missed a few details; it has been some years since I got the letter and check after being tracked down. I burned the letter one night when I was piss-ass drunk, feeling all down and out about how I have never belonged or was never really loved. That is until I meet Xan and his family, they always made me feel like I belonged. They are the only people I've let get close to me knowing how disposable I truly am. If you don't let people in, then they can't leave and hurt you.

I hand Justin his beer and plop back down in my seat, determined to not let my shitty childhood memories bring me down tonight. This is where having a friend to shoot the shit with comes in handy, and why it has sucked so much not having Xan around lately. They keep your mind off of things you don't want to weigh you down. It's nights like this I would always find myself either at Xan's house or balls deep in whatever women I brought home from the bar. The bar's closed for the holidays, so finding a willing female wasn't an option, and Xan is too busy with his new life. So, I replaced him. Not really, I am happy he found Maddie, but I miss hanging out with Xan, shooting the shit. We watch the rest of the movie in silence. Neither of us had anything else to say. Justin doesn't want to talk about his past and I sure as fuck don't want to talk about mine. Hell, I don't even want to think about it.

"I'm gonna head out," Justin says, looking down at his watch. "It's a quarter after twelve."

"Your momma gonna be pissed you missed curfew?" I tease.

"Fuck off, asshole." He spats standing up to leave. When a nasty storm came through, determined to take out our little town, it tore off part of the roof of his house. He has been so busy fixing everyone else's places he hasn't gotten his livable again yet, so he has been crashing with his parents until he can. Even though it is a valid reason, it doesn't mean I can't fuck with him.

"How much longer 'til your back in your own place?" I ask, getting to my feet to see him out and lock up behind him.

"Not much more. I'll be out there working on it tomorrow. The roof's repaired. Now I just have to fix the weather damage to the inside and by all new…" His sentence dies off when we hear a knock at the door. "I guess I picked the perfect time to leave. Your 'booty service call' has arrived." He teases, chuckling at his joke.

"No one was coming over tonight," I reply, looking at the door in confusion as someone bangs on my door again. He glances out of the peephole, then looks back at me with a smirk.

"She's cute. If you're too drunk to get the job done, man… I can take her home with me," Justin offers as I go to open the door.

"Yeah, because all women wish to sneak in and out of a grown man's childhood window," I joke as I open my door to a face, I never thought I would see again. "Brandy." I hiss out, narrowing my eyes at her. I left her behind a little over four years ago in New Orleans. She said if I walked out that door, I would never see her ass again and that is what I was banking on. Now here she stands on my doorstep, bleached out stringy hair all a mess, looking even more strung out now than she did when I left.

"Hi, Jack." She whispers, looking down at her feet.

"What the fuck are you doing here?" I all but seethe in her face. This one right here is why I don't do relationships. After she repeatedly cheated on me, I decided that shit was just not for me. I should have known if my parents thought I was disposable, the women in my life would too.

"Um, well, I wanted you to meet someone." She says, pushing a little girl toward me. I hadn't noticed her or the bags at Brandy's feet until now. She is a beautiful little girl, maybe two or three years old at most. Curly, sandy blond hair, with gray eyes, long lashes, and freckles scattered across her cheeks and nose. She's adorable.

"This is JoAnn Isabell Fisher; I call her Jo. She's your daughter." I can't help but laugh at that, which pisses Brandy off to the high heavens. Her face is turning a bright shade of red.

"Yeah, I'm just gonna leave." I hear Justin mumble as he walks past me, heading to his truck.

"What the fuck are you playing at, Brandy? Are you looking for money or something? A place to hide from whatever shit you got yourself into. What?" I am starting to lose my cool at this point. There is no way I am going to let this bitch try to pull one over on me after the shit she put me through in New Orleans. I am fairly sure she slept her way through the city. There is no way she would know that is my kid and I am not taking her word for it.

She huffs, crossing her arms over her chest, looking down. I notice the little girl looking between the two of us. She looks scared out of her mind. I decide I need to lower my voice and as much as I don't want this bitch in my house, this little girl needs to get out of the cold.

"Come in before she freezes out here, but you can't stay here." She rolls her eyes, pushing past me, bags in hand like she didn't hear a word I just said. No sooner has the door shut when Brandy spins on me, pointing her finger in the center of my chest.

"Don't you tell me who the father is! I think I would know since the kid came out of me, for Christ's sake. And for the record, I don't have any plans to stay in this town, much less with you. I'm just passing through." She stomps off to the love seat, slinging the bags down and directing the girl to sit. Picking up the remote, she turns the channel to some cartoons. Then stomps off to my fridge, pulling out the milk and pouring it into a sippy cup for the kid. Coming back, she sets it down and starts digging through the bags.

"What the hell are you doing? If you're just passing through, then why all the bags? Oh, and maybe check with the other guy you were fucking. If you are looking for a dad, it's not me." She finds what she was digging for and shoves the papers at me.

"Look for yourself, mister *'I know everything'* She's not his. The DNA test proves it and it's why he left me. Said he wasn't raising no snot-nosed brat that belonged to another man." Looking down at the papers in my hand, I see she is telling the truth, at least about him not being the dad, but that doesn't mean I am.

"This doesn't prove she's mine," I say, slinging the papers down at her feet and heading to grab me another beer. I was taking a long swig from my beer when she throws her hands up in the air.

"Take a fucking test then jackass, I don't give a damn if you believe me or not."

"Then why are you here?" I snap at her; she is working my last nerve.

"To give you your fucking kid, do with her what you will. I'm done. This life is not something I want anymore. Being a mom is not something I was cut out for, period. She's yours. You can have her, keep her, give her away, frankly I don't give a fuck what you do, so long as I'm not stuck with her." Her tone is cold and unfeeling. I damn near threw my beer bottle at the crazy bitch. Never in my life have I wanted to hurt a woman, but right now, at this moment, I could throttle this one. Looking over my shoulder and seeing that little girl's eyes fill with tears, at the hateful words her mom just spoke, damn near rips my heart out of my chest. I'm sure she didn't quite understand everything Brandy said, but she understands enough that you can see it break her tiny heart in two.

"What the fuck Brandy?" I yell in her face. There is no way she could truly be this heartless, is there?

"Don't try acting all high and mighty with me. You don't know what it's like being a single parent, especially when you never wanted to be one in the first place. Look, if you don't want her fine, put her up for adoption. I just thought giving your shitty luck with all that, you would want to spare her from the same fate." What the fuck is wrong with this woman? My head is pounding now. How can someone be this heartless?

"You can't be serious right now," I say, shaking my head in disbelief.

"I can and I am, everything she needs is in that bag, I'll give you two weeks to decide if you want to keep her, which at that point I will sign over all parental rights to you, and if not to you then to someone else, either way, doesn't matter to me." She turns around and walks out my front door, never once looking back. Not one ounce of remorse for the crying little girl sitting in my living room left with someone she has never met. What has my life become? I pace the kitchen, picking my phone up and sitting it back down over and over again. It's too late to call anyone right now. I will have to figure out all of this mess by myself, at least until the morning. I can't believe this shit is really happening to me right now. What the fuck do I do now? I never wanted to be a dad, especially like this, with the mom absent. That little girl deserves better than this, better than me. Even if I am her dad, which who the hell knows if I am, I can never be what she needs. I don't know the first thing about being a father. I'm pacing my living room now like a caged animal, with no clue how to calm this poor little girl, or how to care for her.

"It's okay, little one. We will get this all sorted out." I say softly, crouching down in front of her. She looks up at me, sniffling.

"Mommy w-w-w-weft m-m-me." She stutters out, wrapping herself in a hug. God, this tiny thing is breaking me, simply ripping my heart out. I scoop her up in my arms, holding her tight to my chest.

"I know, baby girl, I know. But it's going to be okay, I promise, I'm here. I'll take care of you. Everything will be fine." She blinks her eyes, looking up at me, holding her pinky finger up in my face.

"Pinky promise? You can't break a pinky promise." She says with a furrowed brow. I smile down at her, wrapping my pinky around hers.

"Pinky promise, little one." At this moment, looking into her little eyes, I notice the specks of blue mixed in with her gray, just like mine. Could she be mine? Fuck my life. What have I done? I am not ready to be a dad, much less a full-time single dad. That is not something I ever picture for myself. I am going to fail her. It's as simple as that. She will have a terrible childhood, just like I did, and it will be all my fault. I am going to end up ruining this precious little girl's life.

Chapter 2

JACK

JoJo has stopped crying, for now anyway. I gave her a new nickname, hoping that it will help keep her mind off of her mom. So far, so good. She has been going between watching cartoons and running from one end of the house to the other. The problem is, I don't know how to be a dad. I don't have the slightest clue where to start or what she even needs. Then there is the whole *'Is she even really mine?'* which I'm having trouble wrapping my brain around. If she is, why would Brandy wait until she was three to tell me about her? Although, according to her birth certificate, the dates line up. I noticed a car seat beside my front door about an hour ago, when I looked out to see that she did actually abandon her own kid. It had a note stuck to it with a list of things JoJo likes. Chicken nuggets, mac and cheese, grilled cheese, and chocolate milk. She doesn't like vegetables, and she is not allergic to anything. That's good to know. She didn't leave a way to get ahold of her or say where she was going. How do you just walk away from your kid? I never understood how anyone could do that. I can feel my anger starting to build all over again.

"I'm hungry." JoJo's small voice breaks me out of my thoughts. Fuck, I didn't even think to ask if she had eaten. I had just assumed, with it being almost one in the morning when they showed up, that she would have already fed her dinner. Squatting down to be eye level with her, I reply.

"Come on, little one, let's go find you something to eat, then get you settled for the night." Her eyes light up when I pull out frozen chocolate chip waffles. It's the only thing I have here that she may eat. Thankfully, I had milk still in the fridge. I guess we need to go grocery shopping in the morning. A lot of things will have to be bought if she is going to be here. She will need a bed for starters, toys, clothes, and fuck, what else does a three-year-old need? Step one, feed her, then put her down for the night. Well, I guess a nap, in this case, seeing as it is almost two in the morning now. Step two, get some much-needed advice from Maddie. As soon as I am sure they are awake, I will call them.

She absolutely loved her waffles; however, it took longer to wash all the syrup out of her curly hair than it did to cook and eat them. I didn't think I would ever get her hair clean, and then I had to pry her out of the tub. She turns into a mermaid, her words, not mine when she gets in the water, and she didn't want to get out. By the time I pried her out, it was almost three in the morning, and way past bedtime for someone so tiny to still be up. Finally, I got her settled on the couch and asleep. I do not know how I'm going to do this alone. She hasn't even been here a full day and already I feel overwhelmed. Who is going to stay with her while I work? She can't hang out at the tattoo shop all night. It wouldn't be safe for her, nor would it be professional for us. I'm going to need a babysitter that won't mind staying until twelve or one in the morning when I get in from work. Then there's the problem of not having all the things she needs, like clothes, toys, a bed, hell, even a room. Although there are three rooms in this trailer, I can always turn one into a room for her. Right now, one is full of exercise equipment and the other is just empty. I may need to put a lock on the one with the equipment, so she doesn't go in there and get hurt. Or get a shed for it all and give her a playroom. Hell, I am getting ahead of myself. I still don't know for sure if she is mine or not. *One step at a time, Jack. One step at a time.*

I DIDN'T GET A WINK OF SLEEP. I KEPT GETTING UP TO make sure JoJo was okay, and also to check to see if I had just been dreaming that she was dropped off. Since I wasn't getting any sleep, I watched some YouTube videos to find out how to install the car seat into my truck. It was easy enough and is now all set up, ready for us to go see Maddie and Xan when JoJo wakes up. I started to call them, but I'm sure they would think I was just pulling a prank on them or some shit. I do that sometimes; what can I say? I like to have fun. I guess all that is about to change. It's almost eight o'clock and I am running out of things to do to keep myself busy. Is it too early to wake her up after she was up so late last night? Surely that would help her go to bed earlier tonight, though, right? I only have a moment to ponder over what to do when I hear a tiny whimper coming from the living room, pulling me out of my thoughts. Quickly, I make my way to her. I notice her puffy little eyes and red nose. She has been crying again. Sitting down beside her, I scoop her little body up in my arms, holding her to my chest.

"What's the matter, Little Bit?" I ask, rubbing her back as I rock her on the couch.

"Mommy weft." Sniffling between sobs, she asks. "She no come back, is she?" Her tiny, whispered question rips my heart from my chest. I don't want to lie to her, but I am also sure she isn't ready for the truth. Truth is, I don't know if she will ever come back, but if I had to guess, I don't think she is.

"I don't know, Little Bit," I whisper against the top of her head before placing a soft kiss. "But I tell you what, we are going to go see my brother and his fiancée for a little while. They have two kids. They are a little older than you, but I'm sure they would love to meet you. How does that sound?" Her tiny face lights up at the mention of other kids and she jumps out of my arms.

"Let's go, hurry." She says, walking towards the door. I can't help but laugh at her excitement.

"Don't you think you need to go pee in the potty first and

change into your big girl panties and some warmer clothes? I think it's too cold outside to leave in a nightgown." Huffing out a breath and rolling her eyes, she heads to the bathroom. God. I hope I'm doing this right. One of the notes I found in her bag said she was potty training and to only put a pull up on her at night. I don't know if that included when leaving the house as well. Maybe I should take some extra clothes with us to be on the safe side. Brandy had me scratching my head this morning when I started rifling through the bags she packed. I was looking to make sure there were no needles or anything since you could clearly tell she was still using. Instead, I found notes about JoJo. They looked to be just scribbled down quickly as if the thoughts had entered her mind while packing or maybe even during the drive down here. Explaining JoJo's likes and dislikes, her potty training and what to do, her favorite cartoons and toys, and even foods she will eat. I have notes on just about anything I could have thought to ask. It left me wondering if she cared enough to write the notes, then how did she not care enough to keep her? That was until I found the note stating that she tried to think of anything I would need to know, so there was no reason for me to bother her, other than to sign the papers so she could move on with her life, kid-free. The pounding started in my head again.

When JoJo's done in the bathroom, I help her get cleaned up and brush her teeth, then we head back to the living room to pick out something to wear for the day. We packed up some extra clothes to take with us just in case we need them. After she's dressed, and we have the to-go bag packed, I wash her sippy cup and fill it with the last of the milk I have. We will have to stop for breakfast since there is nothing else here to feed her. I tell her to watch some cartoons while I walk out into the cold to warm up my truck and put her little backpack in with a few toys to keep her occupied while we are out today. She is the sweetest little thing; I smile at her as I walk back in, seeing her dance while singing along with Elmo. I really hope her mom walking out on her as she did doesn't leave lasting negative effects on her. She deserves so much better than all of this shit.

"You ready to go, Little Bit?" I ask holding her jacket up for her by the door. She spins around, her curls falling in front of her face as she does.

"Yep," she answers with a big smile on her face, holding her doll close as she makes her way over to me. After we get her jacket on, I pick her up, ready to leave. Before we can even make it out of the door, she squeals, almost bursting my eardrum in the process.

"Wait!!! Baby needs blankie." She says, holding her baby doll up to my face to show me who she is referring to. I chuckle, shaking my head.

"Ok, let's find her a blankie." After looking all over for something to use as a blankie, we settle on a clean towel. I guess that's something else I will need to get, and soon. Who knew someone so small would need so much stuff? Finally, I have her in her seat and buckled up. First stop, get food, second stop, ask Maddie for help, and finally off to the store to get the things I will need to care for her until her mom comes back. If she ever comes back, I am only kidding myself thinking she will. Heaven help me, I am so far out of my depth here.

We pull up to a little diner in town to grab some breakfast. I can't help but notice the strange looks I keep getting. No doubt, everyone is curious as to who trusted a fuck up like me with their precious little girl. I might be being a little too hard on myself. I'm not a bad guy, I don't get into trouble with the law. Except for the one time, that woman's old man showed up as I was plowing into her. In my defense, I didn't know they were back together. She had told me they were getting a divorce. I don't purposely cause problems for people. I've held down a steady job for years, and own my home, even if it is small. Still, I'm not parent material. I don't have a clue how to do this. I didn't have the best of examples growing up and kids don't come with an instruction manual. Not that I would read it, anyway. When has anyone ever seen a man read the instruction manual? Even with the judging looks coming from the other customers, no one asks any questions, and we enjoy our breakfast in silence. While we eat, my thoughts drift to Maddie and Xan, I hope that they can help me figure out how to handle all the things that have been thrown my way overnight.

After we pulled up to Xan and Maddie's house and I helped JoJo down from my truck. We head up to the front door, knocking, we wait for someone to answer. Out of all the people that could have answered the door, Harley was not the person I expected or the one I wanted to see. Could today get any worse?

We couldn't get along if our lives depended on it. She is always snapping at me for every little thing I say and do. Most days I enjoy the game, the back and forth with this beautiful woman, wait did I just think that? I must be more sleep-deprived than I thought. Today, though, I just don't have it in me. There is just too much on my mind at the moment. Here goes nothing. I let my best smirk fall into place.

Chapter 3

HARLEY

SITTING HERE AT MADDIE'S, I HAVE FOUND MYSELF having more fun than I have in a while. I jumped at the opportunity to watch Sammie and Seth for Maddie, so she and Xander could go buy furniture for the nursery. They are so excited about the new little addition to their family and just couldn't wait to start decorating, and as for me, well... I have missed these two kids more than I thought was possible since they moved in over here. We have spent most of the morning playing board games and laughing until our stomachs hurt. I needed this. It has been way too quiet at home lately and lonely, so fucking lonely. I thought that the bills alone were going to be the hardest part, but I was wrong. The hardest part is not having my best friend and my two favorite kids around me all the time. Don't get me wrong, I am thrilled that Maddie found love and is happy. I just hate being by myself all the time. I need to find a roommate or a second job, not only to be able to afford the ever-growing stack of bills, but also to keep myself busy.

Not staying busy leads to too much thinking. Too much thinking leads to depression, and no one has time for that, certainly not me. We will not dwell on any of that right now. Today is meant to be fun, and that is precisely what it will be. We were just starting a game of UNO when we hear a knock at the door.

"I wonder if mom and dad are back already?" Sammie asks.

"Why would they knock?" Seth points out as I get up from my spot on the floor and head to the door. I love that Xander is so good with the twins, and they took to him with no problem. Even started calling him dad shortly after they moved in with him. They never knew their dad, so Xander is the closest thing they have ever had. All kids deserve two have loving parents. And even though I am painfully aware that sometimes that isn't how life works, I'm thrilled that they now have two amazing parents instead of just one. I open the door to see Jackass, aka Jack, Xander's best friend, and a royal pain in my ass. My good mood instantly morphs into annoyance.

"Look at what the cat dragged in," I say with a huff crossing my arms and lean against the door frame. Don't get me wrong. I'm not trying to say that I don't find Jack to be extremely fucking hot, because I do. How could I not? I have eyes. I'm 5'7 and he easily towers over me, with his broad shoulders, a muscular chest that tapers into a trim waist, down to his tree-trunk legs. His brown hair is always styled in a way that screams just fucked, and his amazing gray/blue eyes could keep you mesmerized for days. Oh, and let's not forget all the lickable tattoos covering his body. His stretched ears even look good on him. Basically, everything about him physically makes me hot. I don't even typically like facial hair and yet his neatly trimmed beard looks like the perfect seat, if you know what I mean. The problem with him is, that he is, and has always been, a complete asshole. From the moment I met him in foster care when I was ten, he has felt the need to make fun of my name, and it drives me insane. I know I can't hold something he did as a stupid teenager against him, and maybe I wouldn't if he didn't continue to do so now. The first time I saw him as an adult, I admittedly acted like a bitch and gave him the cold shoulder when he was flirting with me, but damn, those horrible four months in foster care came right back the moment my eyes landed on him. He had the audacity to act as he had never met me before. Granted, we were just kids and not in this town, but come on, how many Harleys do you know? I'll never forget that night I came face to face with the fucker again after all those years. Xander had a fourth of July party earlier this year and they invited me to come along with Maddie and the twins, but to my surprise, I come face to face with none other than Jackass himself. He tried to shake my hand in greeting, and I brushed by him with a roll of my eyes. Now, I know petty, but I just couldn't get all the jokes out of my head that he threw my way when we were kids. Then he preceded to continually try and flirt with me like he had no clue who I was. I honestly think he still doesn't remember me. I have even tried to drop hints to see if he would react, but nothing. So, here we are now adults and still bickering like we are tweens.

"If it isn't little miss Shadow, to what do I owe the pleasure?" He purrs back at me, dragging his eyes down the length of my body. The action makes me shiver and I hope to everything holy he doesn't notice it. The smirk that graces his full, kissable lips tells me that he did indeed notice and it thrilled him. Damn it and damn my treacherous body for reacting.

"Xander's not here, so you can leave now," I say as I start to close the door in his face. He stops it with a big boot.

"I'm here to see Maddie." He says raising a brow as he starts to push through the door. I hold my hands up to stop him.

"She's not here either. Besides, what could you need with her?" He looks down behind his leg and it's just then I notice the tiny blonde girl clinging to him for dear life.

"I need some advice." He says, gesturing to the little girl. "We can wait here for them to get back. I thought maybe the twins could help keep her company for a while." I can't help myself. Being a bitch to this man is second nature.

"Who was stupid enough to trust a man-child like you with a precious little thing like her?" I ask as I crouch down at eye level with her. When she locks eyes with me, it knocks the air right out of my lungs. I would know those eyes anywhere; I have fantasied about them enough in my life. Dear God, he has a kid. I pop back to standing so fast it makes me dizzy.

"Since when do you have a kid?" I hiss, my eyes as big as saucers.

"Apparently, for three years now, just heard about it a little after midnight. Besides, we have no proof yet. That's just what her mom says. I'll have to take a DNA test to be sure." I snort out a laugh, causing him to stop talking. He's now looking at me like he could kill me at any moment. "Something funny?" He asks, crossing his enormous arms over his chest.

"I can tell you without a DNA test, she is yours. She looks just like you. When will her mom be back?" I ask as I open the door for them to walk in. No matter how much I hate this man, I refuse to let this little girl freeze because of it. Dread fills me when I see the scared shitless look cross his face. Not because I don't think he could make a wonderful dad if he wanted that in life, but because my heart hurts for this little girl. He quickly introduces her as JoJo to the twins and turns on some cartoons for her, then sits her on the couch before he motions for me to follow him into the kitchen. With every step I take behind him, I feel a weight pressing down on my heart.

"I don't think she will be coming back." He whispers, shaking his head. "Brandy showed up saying JoJo was mine and now my problem to deal with, that she was done and never wanted to be a mom. I questioned whether she was just going through something. I thought maybe she just wanted money or a break, but then when I started going through her bags to see what all I might need while she was here, I found these." He says, pulling some folded papers from his back pocket, handing them to me. I quickly skim over them only to realize that they are custody papers already drawn up to sign over all rights to Jack. He collapses into a chair, drops his head, and buries his fingers into his hair. I can't stop myself before I know it, I'm smoothing my hand up and down his back trying to comfort him.

"You won't believe what the bitch said." He mumbles. I'm scared to ask but don't have to, he tells me anyway. "She told me she didn't care if I kept her or just gave her away, as long as she didn't have to keep her. The only reason she came to me was because I had told her how bad foster care was and she thought I would want to save JoJo from the pain. How do you just walk away from your kid like that?" *That poor little girl.* "Does she not realize that walking away is hurting her, too?" He asks, shaking his head.

"Sometimes the kid is better off in the long run if the shitty parent walks away," I answer, thinking back to my childhood. Even if foster care sucked those few months before my grandmother adopted me, it was leaps and bounds better than being drug from one filthy hotel room to the next with my crack whore of mom. A sad smile graces his handsome face.

"I know." He says so low I barely hear him before he gets to his feet, walking to the kitchen entrance, he peeks into the living room at the kids watching cartoons. Sammie is holding JoJo in her lap, playing with her hair, and I see a genuine smile on his face. "Maddie has the best kids." He says more to himself. "I hope I can do at least half as good a job as she has." My hand rests on his shoulder as I step closer to him.

"I'm sure you will." His eyes meet mine and for a moment, the air between us seems to sizzle. Then he opens his big stupid mouth.

"Thanks, Shadow, that means a lot." He says, placing a hand over his heart like my words touched him in some way. And just like that, the mood's broken. I punch him as hard as I can in the shoulder, causing him to laugh while he rubs the spot I hit.

"Wow, someone is touchy today." He throws over his shoulder as he saunters back to the kids. I can't fucking stand that asshole. Clenching my fist by my side, I let out a growl of frustration before I walk out of the kitchen. *You will not let him see that his words get to you, Harley.* I mentally give myself a much-needed pep talk to get through the rest of this unfortunate visit. Head held high and my best-unfazed look plastered on my face, I walk back into the living room. I don't want to interrupt Maddie and Xander's shopping, but I really hope they get back home soon so I can leave. My good time with my favorite kids has officially ended, thanks to Sir Jackass himself.

We make it through lunch with the kids, without me killing Jack. It's a miracle. It takes more restraint than I knew I had, but we made it. I'm almost squealing with relief when Maddie walks in.

"Good Jack, I'm glad you're here. You can go help Xander bring in all the heavy stuff." She says with a huge smile on her face as she sits her bag and keys down on the entry table, then hangs her coat up in the closet.

"Anything for my favorite girl," Jack says, placing a kiss on her cheek as he walks by her, heading out the door to help Xander.

"Well, I'm surprised he's here, and still alive, for that matter. Who is this?" She asks, confusion etched across her face.

"This is JoJo, Jack's daughter." Sammie declares like everyone should have already known this information, as she cuddles the little girl closer to her. Maddie shoots me a questioning look.

"Well, it's nice to meet you, JoJo." She coos, kneeling in front of the little girl. JoJo smiles up at Maddie.

"How about Harley and I go make you guys a snack?" Maddie says quickly, standing to her feet and making her way to the kitchen, signaling for me to follow her. Once I enter the kitchen, she spins on me.

"What? Jack has a kid. Since when?" She asks, looking hurt that she didn't already know this. I know she has gotten close to Jack since she and Xander have been together. I'm sure it hurts her feelings, thinking she's the very last to know that someone she now views as part of her family had a secret kid.

"He apparently just found out last night when her mom dumped her off on him," I answer, trying again not to cry for the poor little girl. Maddie, on the other hand, doesn't succeed, with her hormones all over the place. The tears flow freely from her eyes.

"How could a mom do that?" She asks cradling her barley there, baby bump in her hands. She was lucky to grow up, with two always present parents, who loved her unconditionally and still do. I imagine something such as this would be hard for her to wrap her mind around.

"Some people just aren't cut out to be parents, I guess," I say with a shrug of my shoulder. She is still sniffling back tears when Xander and Jack walk in.

"I see you told Maddie," Jack says as he leans against the wall, crossing his arms over his chest. Xander wraps Maddie in a hug.

"Don't cry Angel, I'm positive she will be much better off without someone in her life who is willing to throw her away like that." He smooths her hair out of her face, gently placing a kiss on her temple. If that is not some of the truest words, I have ever heard.

"He's right," I say at the same time Jack says.

"Amen to that." I look over to see the sad look in his eyes. As much as he grates my nerves, we have more in common than I would like to admit.

"So, what's the plan, then? How do we manage this moving forward?" Maddie asks, wiping the tears from her face, and pulling her shoulders back, ready to save the day. Jack chuckles, pushing away from the wall.

"So, are you saying you are going to finally admit to Xander that the bundle of joy you are carrying is mine? Move-in with me so we can raise all these kids together?" He jokes with a smile on his face, earning him a slap to the back of the head from Xander and a laugh from Maddie.

"No." She giggles, snuggling deeper into Xander. "But we are family, and we will get through this together. What do you need? We will help in any way we can." She tells him. She has always been like this. Ready to do whatever she can to help the people she loves, and I love her for it.

"I know you will." Jack sighs, sitting down at the table. "I need to get a DNA test for one, make sure she's protected above all else. Then there is so much to do at my place. She will need a bed, toys, more clothes, a doctor, hell I don't even know what all she will need. I don't know how to do this. That's why I came to you." Jack huffs, hanging his head in defeat again.

"I will help make sure everything is bought and set up for her Jack, don't worry about that," Maddie says, wrapping an arm around his shoulder.

"How will I be able to go to work? She can't stay at home alone. This is all such a mess." Jack whispers, locking eyes with Xander. Maddie looks at me and I can see her brain at work. I shake my head no before she can even speak. Does that stop her? Fuck no, it doesn't, traitor.

"Harley, weren't you just saying the other day how you missed having the twins around and a roommate?" My eyes go wide and I'm shaking my head so hard it's giving me a headache. She continues, not to be deterred. "You should move in with Jack, then you can keep JoJo while he is at work. It's perfect!" She exclaims, clasping her hands together. I snort out a nervous laugh.

"How is that perfect? We can't stand each other." I say, pointing between Jack and me.

"That would work," Jack says out of nowhere. "Come on, Scooter, we won't even see each other all that much. We work different hours." I snap my eyes over to him; I know he can see the rage in my eyes because he flinches slightly at it.

"Are you fucking insane? We are always at each other's throats. It would be a disaster. For God's sake, you can't even manage to get my name right, much less be civil with me." I all but shout, throwing my hands up in the air. "Nope, no way, hell fucking no. I love you Maddie, but you have lost your ever-loving mind if you think that could ever work. I've got to go; see you later." Spinning on my heels, I rush out the door. I can't be a part of this crazy shit show.

Maddie is calling my name from the porch as I shut my car door, but I can't stay and talk. Before I have a full panic attack, I have to get out of here. I can't do this again. Even if Jack and I got along perfectly, I can't help raise another kid. I can't watch another baby grow into an amazing little kid, knowing I can never have that experience myself. It was one thing when it was Maddie's kids, hard, yes, but doable because they are my pseudo niece and nephew. Helping Jack would be too much. She wouldn't have a mom around. She would come to me for all the mom things until he decided to settle down, then I would lose her to some other woman. My heart aches just thinking about it while tears burn at the back of my eyes. There is no way in hell I could survive that, just no way. He is on his own with this one. They will have to find someone else, simple as that. My poor heart has been through enough and simply can't handle that amount of pain.

Chapter 4

HARLEY

I AM SITTING IN THE LIVING ROOM WATCHING THE CABIN in The Woods with a pint of Rocky Road in hand, trying to forget that being a mom is something I will probably never experience when my phone pings with a text alert. Looking down, I sigh when I see a text from Jack. Why can't he just leave me alone?

> Jackass: Why did you run out like that Shadow? Living with me wouldn't be that bad. I could make it worth your while.

I roll my eyes, dropping my spoon into the carton so I can reply.

> Me: You have nothing I want that could make dealing with you worth my time.

He takes no time at all to text back.

> Jackass: That's where you are wrong my dear, see I happen to know, thanks to Maddie, you are struggling to pay the bills alone. She feels terrible by the way, since she moved out on you, essentially leaving you in a bind. Now here is where I come in. I need someone who I can trust to be at home with JoJo while I work. I plan to have a house built on the front of my property, if you move in and help me out, and even continue to watch her while I am at work after the house is built, I will give you the single wide free and clear.

> Jackass: You can even keep it on my land.

> Jackass: You can't possibly pass up such an amazing deal.

My mouth falls open. I have to read his messages four times to be sure I read them right. He is certifiably crazy. That's all I can come up with.

> Me: Have you lost your ever-loving mind?

I can't believe he thinks he can buy me like this. He has to be high or something. Although I mean, it's not a terrible deal. No Harley, no, you are smarter than that don't fall for his trap.

> Jackass: Come on Scooter, what do you have to lose? JoJo needs someone who is good with kids to be with her while I work. I know you will take good care of her.

> Me: And when you meet someone and settle down, then what, I just walk away and never have anything to do with her again? That would break her heart. Also, do you think whatever woman you move in with you will be ok with me living so close? I think not. I'd have to move and then be right back to square one.

Seriously, there's no way he has thought this through all the way.

> Jackass: Not a chance in hell. I will never be settling down. I won't even bring anyone home to JoJo, I'll go to them. No need to confuse her like that. Besides, this is all assuming that I am indeed her dad. I still have to take the test.

> Me: You know she's yours, and you're not letting her go anywhere.

> Jackass: You're right, the Little Monster has warmed her way into my heart. SO.... Is that a yes to helping us?

> Me: Can I have some time to think about it, please? Without you hounding me over it.

> Jackass: Absolutely Scooter. We won't open the shop back up until after the first. You think you can have an answer by then?

> Me: Yeah, bye now.

> Jackass: Bye

I can't believe I am even thinking about going through with this crazy plan. How dare he use me needing a home that I can afford, and that beautiful curly-headed girl against me like that? He has to know I have a soft spot for kids, especially since she will need a mother figure in her life.

'Stop, Harley, you can't start thinking of yourself as a mom for her. It's not anywhere close to being like that. You will be nothing more than a live-in nanny until they build his house, and a babysitter after that,' I silently tell myself. Never forget your place in all of this. All you will get is a broken heart if you do.

I drop my phone next to me, flopping my head back against the cushion. There is no way this is going to end well for me. I can't seem to get into my movie now and my ice cream has been completely forgotten. My stomach is in knots. I want to talk to Maddie about all of this, but she still doesn't know what the doctors told me. Hell, only one other person who knows I miscarried and that the doctors said too much scar tissue was left behind after the infection that my chances of conceiving and carrying to full term are slim. That's why Rhett left, well, that and his secretary, but that is a story for another day. I don't want to think about it all right now. Maybe a good nap will help clear up all of my options for me.

It's been a week since I last spoke to Jack. One week to make the hardest decision in my life, well, one of the hardest. A week of watching my unpaid bills pile up on my kitchen table. Another week of calling and begging yet again for an extension on my power bill, so it doesn't get cut off. A week of me realizing just how much I do need help. The more I think about it, the better the deal with Jack sounds. Perhaps we can make it work. For the sake of that little girl, we can get along. With any hope, this won't be the worst decision of my life. Only second to the day I said "I do" to that piece of shit Rhett. Who am I kidding? This is going to be a complete disaster. Am I still seriously considering it, even knowing this can't possibly work out? Yes, yes, I am. I pull Jack's text thread up before I can chicken out and send him a text.

> Me: If I say yes to this crazy idea of yours, we will have to have something in writing stating that I not only get the trailer, but that I also can keep it where it is for as long as I need. I don't want to be left in a situation where I can be evicted just because you get pissed off at me.

I press send and drop the phone on the table by my unpaid, extremely late stack of bills. I'm so beyond stressed out and have no clue what I am going to do if he has changed his mind or if he found someone else to take my place. An hour passes before my phone chimes with a response. A full hour of me pacing my kitchen, wondering where I went wrong in life. I snatch up my phone to see what kind of smart-ass reply he has for me today, preparing myself fully to have an equally bitchy reply. Only his reply isn't a smartass reply. It is... hell, I don't even know.

> Jackass: Anything you need. Do you know anyone who could write up a contract, or do you want to just do one between the two of us?

I was not expecting that. Honestly, I was expecting him to dig in his heels, just to be a pain in my ass even though this was all his idea.

> Me: Just between us is fine. I'll type up something and send it to you tomorrow. Once we have agreed on everything, we can move forward. If you feel you need to add anything, do so and send it back to me to review.

> Jackass: Sounds good and thank you. You do not know how much this makes me feel better about going back to work. I've got to go. Time to do this test. My email is jackwilliams@XansINK.com. Shoot it on over and I will go over it as soon as I can.

That's it, no calling me Shadow, or Scooter, didn't even give me a hard time, and he even thanked me. I don't think I have ever heard the man say thank you to anyone, ever. Didn't even know the words were in his vocabulary. I spend the rest of my day writing up a contract for us, going by a mock one I found online, with all the rules I expect to be followed while I am living with him, as well as the ones I expect to be followed after his house is built and I take over the trailer permanently. After I'm finished, I send it to him. Then I start making a list of what I plan to take with me, what will go into storage and what I will donate. As well as a list of things to ask Maddie if she wants. Then I make a list of all the things I need to call and cancel, along with making a note to remember to message Bob and let him know when I will be moving, so he can rent this place to someone else. Once all that is done, I collapse onto my favorite chair and try not to freak the fuck out over the decision I have made. What could possibly go wrong, other than every fucking thing?

Chapter 5

JACK

I was sitting in my bed relaxing, after a long day of finishing up JoJo's room and having the DNA test done. We will have results in two to four business days. Then I can officially take full custody of JoJo and not have to worry about Brandy taking her away from me. When my email pinged, alerting me that Harley had sent me her contract, I opened it up to read it. All these rules were not what I was expecting. I was honestly thinking it was going to be just for the trailer, not all of this.

I, Jackson Williams, agree to sign over the deed to my 3-bedroom 2-bath single-wide trailer, to one Harley Gains after I build my house. Given that she stays at my home in the meantime as a live-in nanny for my daughter. After which she will own the trailer and has my full permis-

sion to keep the above-mentioned trailer on my land, even given the chance that we have a falling out, for as long as she may need. I, nor anyone else, can make her move her person, or the trailer, off my land for any reason. Below is a list of rules for both parties to follow during the time Harley Gains is residing in Jackson Williams's home, as well as after, for as long as she resides on his land, continuing the care of his daughter.

Rules are as followed to be added to, and, or, taken away from, only as agreed upon by both parties.

1. *Neither Jackson, nor Harley, are allowed to bring in a partner during the time Harley resides in the home, to prevent conflict for either party or unnecessary confusion for the child.*
2. *Both Jackson and Harley are to remain fully dressed at all times, when outside of their respective bedrooms and/or bathrooms.*
3. *Harley is to have her own room and to only share a bathroom with the child.*

4. *Jackson is to respect Harley, calling her only by her given name at any point in time, nicknames will not be permitted.*
5. *Harley is to respect any rules set forth by Jackson for his child at all times but asks that Jackson agree to consider her opinion when it comes to the child's health and well-being.*
6. *If at any point either party decides that it is in the best interest of the child, the contract can be terminated, with plenty of notice for Harley to make other plans for her living arrangements.*
7. *Harley requires no less the one weekend a month off, to leave the home and do what she wishes with her personal time.*
8. *When Jackson is not present in the home, Harley agrees to be the sole provider for the child.*
9. *Harley is only responsible for cooking and cleaning for/and after herself, except when she is providing care for the child, in which case those*

RESPONSIBILITIES EXTEND TO THE CHILD IN QUESTION.

10. *HARLEY IS AGREEING TO PROVIDE CARE FOR THE CHILD WITH NO PAYMENT, OUTSIDE OF OBTAINING OWNERSHIP OF THE TRAILER, AND WILL CONTINUE TO DO SO EVEN WHEN THAT TIME COMES, AND WILL CONTINUE TO PROVIDE CARE FOR THE CHILD AFTER, AS LONG AS SHE IS STILL LIVING ON THE PREMISES.*
11. *JACKSON AGREES TO NEVER HOLD THE CHILD AGAINST HARLEY IF AT ANY POINT HE BECOMES UPSET WITH HARLEY.*
12. *THE CHILD'S HEALTH AND WELL-BEING WILL ALWAYS BE PLACED FIRST BY ALL PARTIES INVOLVED.*
13. *AFTER THE TIME COMES WHEN HARLEY OBTAINS OWNERSHIP OF THE TRAILER, JACKSON AGREES THAT IF IN THE CASE HE BRINGS SOMEONE ELSE IN TO LIVE WITH HIM, HARLEY IS STILL ALLOWED TO LIVE ON THE PREMISES, AND THE OTHER PERSON MAY NOT CAUSE ISSUES WITH HARLEY AT ANY TIME.*

SIGNATURE DATE
x_____ _____
x_____ _____

TILYA ELOFF

I know without question; that she will not bend on any of the rules she has set. They seem silly to me, but if she is willing to help me out, I have to at least try. I will have to let Xan know I will need a weekend off each month after I speak with Harley to find out what weekend would be best for her. One could only hope that Sunday is enough of a break for her since we're closed then anyway, but given the fact that she knows that, and it is still a rule, I have no doubt Sunday is not the day she wants for herself. I send her a quick text, hoping to iron out the day needed as quickly as possible.

> Me: What day of the month works best for you? I need to work it out with Xan.

She doesn't text me back right away, not that I expect anything different. I read back over the contract again, trying to decide if there is anything I want to add, just to be a dick, but can't think of anything. She seemed to have covered everything and aside from me adding something solely to piss her off; I have nothing. As fun as pissing her off is, I refrain from doing so. I really need her here for JoJo and do not want to fuck this up. Knowing I won't hear from her again tonight and JoJo will be up bright and early in the morning, I decide to call it a night. I have a storage building being delivered tomorrow as well, so I can clear out the spare room for Harley.

I find myself yet again, not sure how many times now, dreaming about my years in foster care. All the bullshit and hell I was forced to live through, year after year, home after home.

They were all the same. People who pretended to care about you, but in reality, just wanted the check and the praise they got for taking in the unwanted kids. The last one wasn't that bad, but by the time I made it to them, I was already soured by the entire experience and refused to let them get close to me. I did my time like a good little boy, kept my head down, stayed out of trouble, out of sight, and left as soon as I turned eighteen. Spent the last four months of my senior year living with Xan and Pops. Then, after Xan got himself into trouble and went into the military, I was alone. Jumping from job to job, not sure what I wanted out of life. When Xan called saying he was home and wanted to travel a bit, I jumped at the chance to do so. We ended up in New Orleans. That was home, for a while at least. Both of us thought that was where we belonged. We had settled down with the girls we met there, who were best friends themselves. As luck would have it, they also shared the same addiction. Xander's girl overdosed not long after a falling out they had, and shortly after he moved back home. I wasn't far behind him, officially tired of Brandy's bullshit lies and cheating. Her behavior only got worse after her friend died, but lucky me, I didn't hightail it fast enough.

Is it weird that now that JoJo is in my life, even for as brief as it has been, that I wouldn't change it, any of it for the world? Don't get me wrong, I'm still scared shitless that I'm going to fuck up being a dad for this little girl. But for all the fear I have, I can't help but think the shit I lived through was preparing me for this moment. I already love that little girl with everything I am. She has me completely wrapped around her little finger. I find myself praying now that I am her biological dad, whereas when she first got here, it was the last thing I wanted. I would be devastated if she wasn't and they took her away from me, and I think she would be too. Three days into her being with me, she asked me who I was to her, and what was she supposed to call me. She said her mom said I was her dad and asked if it was okay if she called me daddy. My heart broke a little more for her at that moment. It was then I realized that she had very much listened, taking in everything that Brandy said to me that night. I told her if that is what she wanted to call me, she could, and that I would be honored. I explained the best way I could that we had to do a DNA test and what it was, but no matter what the test said, I would do all I could to always keep her. I know it's too much for a three-year-old little mind, but a part of me worries she won't be mine, and that no matter what I do, they will take her from me. I don't want to fill her with false hope and security until we know for sure what the outcome will be.

"Daddy, my's hungry." I hear her sweet little voice call as she runs through the hall and burst through my door. Blonde curls wild and all over the place, a sleepy smile on her pretty little face. I can't help but smile back at her as I sit up in bed.

"Oh yeah, what do you want for breakfast then, Little Monster?" I ask as I get up and walk over to pick her up.

"My not monster daddy, my princess." She sasses, crossing her arms and trying her best to give me a mean face. This has

ALL OR NOTHING

been our morning; every morning for the past week, and it's getting harder and harder for her to look mad at me. Finally, she breaks and starts laughing. Grabbing my cheeks, she says. "You silly daddy, I want pancakes please." *Ahh.* The dreaded pancakes. She is so messy anytime she has syrup, but if that's what she wants, that's what she will get. I will, however, remember to pull her hair up this time, though.

"Okay Princess, let's go get you fed." We head into the kitchen, opting for frozen pancakes this morning. I have her food made, and she is sitting down, digging in, in no time at all. I take the opportunity to grab a quick shower and get dressed while she eats.

When I am dressed and ready for the day, I head back to the kitchen to get JoJo cleaned up, then wash up the dishes. Finally, I can get some much-needed coffee for myself. I don't see how single moms manage this while also working. I feel like I never have the time I need in a day to get everything done, and still give her the attention she needs. Thankfully, Xan, Maddie, and the twins are coming today to give me a hand with her, while I clean out the room for Harley. I really hope she hasn't changed her mind. Without her help, I don't know what I'll do. I've drained my second cup of coffee when my phone dings with a new text.

> Harley: The second Saturday of the month works for me if y'all can make that work. Did you want to add anything to the contract? Or did you have a problem with any of it?

> Me: I'll talk with Xan, I'm sure we can make that work. Nothing to add, everything looks fine. I have no problem signing.

> Harley: Okay, I guess if everything works for the both of us, we can sign it and go from there. When will you need me moved in?

> Me: As soon as possible so JoJo can get used to you. She's been through enough. I will get the spare room cleaned out today.

> Harley: I guess I'll start moving stuff in tomorrow then if that works for you.

> Me: Sound good.

Placing my phone back into my pocket, I head to the living room to see what JoJo is up to. I find her trying to put a movie into my PS4, upside down.

"What are you doing, Gremlin?" I ask, crouching down beside her.

"Frozen." Is her only reply, as she hands the disk over to me, clearly done trying to figure it out on her own.

"We watched this five times yesterday. Are you sure you want to watch it again?" I ask, hoping I can change her mind.

"Yes daddy, Frozen." I smile down at her pouty face; I can't seem to say no to this girl. Heaven help me when she gets older. It's going to be pure hell. I can see it now.

"Okay, okay, Frozen it is." I chuckle as I place the movie in and get it started for her. She grabs her new Elsa doll and blanket before climbing up on the couch to watch her new favorite movie. In no time mesmerized by TV and she doesn't even notice when I walk out to smoke. Lighting up my cigarette, I take a long drawl. I have missed rolling a blunt and smoking it, but this will have to do now. As long as she is in the house, weed is not. Hell, I even stopped loading my fridge with beers, scared she may get into them. Maybe I can put a fridge in the storage building, so I can still have a drink when I want to.

It is a quarter past nine when the storage building is drooped off, and Xan, Maddie, and the twins aren't too far behind them. Sammie did not even say hey when I answered the door, just rushed right on in, scooping JoJo up in her arms and smothering her with kisses. Maddie just shakes her head, smiling.

"She's been begging all week to come steal her for the day." She says, hugging me.

"How have y'all been?" Xan pats my back as he walks up beside us, before pulling Maddie into his arms, stroking her barely noticeable baby belly.

"Doing good, just exhausted. I don't know how you did it for so long by yourself." Maddie just giggles.

"Well, because I didn't, Harley helped me a lot." The conversation keeps moving as we find ourselves standing in the spare room, Xan holding Maddie to him. The both of them now lovingly caressing her baby bump, without even noticing they are doing it. For the first time since they met, I find myself insanely jealous of my best friend. Love and a relationship have never really been something I have wanted. I am still not entirely sure it is something I would want for myself, but for JoJo, I want everything for her. The entire package—two loving parents and siblings to play with, fight with, and love unconditionality. She deserves to have all of it. Instead, she is stuck with me.

"Hey, what's wrong, man?" Xan asks with one brow raised in confusion.

"Nothing, why?" I ask, not sure if I said something out loud that I did not mean to. Usually, that only happens when I am high or drunk and, unfortunately, I'm stone-cold sober right now.

"I ask you if you were ready to get started. Maddie went to hang with the kids, and you were just staring off into space." He says, crossing his arms over his chest, and props himself up against the wall. "You know, if you need help or even just a break, we're here for you, man. You don't have to do this all on your own." I let out a slow, long breath.

"I know, I know. I was just thinking of all the things I need to get done before tomorrow, so Harley can move her things in." I say, completely deflecting.

"Let's get started then." He says, knowing if he pushes for me to tell him what is bothering me, it will only piss me off.

We spend most of the day moving all of my workout equipment out of the house, only breaking for lunch when Maddie threatened to skin us both alive if we didn't. She might be small, but fuck, she is scary. The sun is going down by the time we are finished, and we collapse onto my patio furniture.

"Damn, man, you have enough stuff to open your own gym. Why the fuck do we pay to go to one?" Xan asks as he reaches into his pocket. I shrug my shoulders, letting my head fall back, looking up at the sky.

"Hell, if I know." My head pops up when the sticky, sweet smell of weed hits my nose. "What the actual fuck man, put that out. The kids are here." I say, reaching for the joint in his hand to put it out myself.

"Chill, man, they're inside with Maddie." He replies, holding it out of my reach. "They could come out." I counter as I start to stand.

"Calm down. If they do, so what? They might ask us what we are doing, and we'll tell them we are having a smoke break. I know you haven't stopped smoking; I saw a full ashtray on the porch." He snatched his hand back when I tried to reach for it again.

"I have to be more responsible now. I have JoJo to think about." Knowing he will not give it to me, I dropped my ass back down. He takes a long pull off of it, holding the smoke in his lungs for a beat before letting it out.

"And what, I'm not responsible? I don't help raise two kids with a third on the way. As long as they have what they need and are cared for, what does it matter if we get a little high at the end of a long day? It's not like I'm asking you to do some hard drugs with me, it's just a little weed. But if it makes you feel better, I will put it out." He goes to do just that when I stop him. He passes it to me, and I inhale deeply. Fuck, I needed this. He's right, it's not like I'm doing anything hard, and JoJo is safe and taken care of. It will not hurt anyone if I get a little buzzed.

We pass the joint back and forth until it's completely gone before either of us speaks again. I should have seen the question coming. I should have been prepared to deflect again. The gears were spinning in his head. I should have known this was his plan all along to get me talking.

"So, you going to tell me what caused you to bug out earlier?" He asks, looking up at the stars. I sigh, pulling a cigarette out of my pack and lighting it.

"She deserves better, man." Is my only response.

"I'm assuming we are talking about JoJo. I hate how her mom left things, but she's better off if you ask me." He declares, still not looking at me.

"It's not just her mom, it's all of it. She deserves to have two parents, siblings, grandparents, and a whole fucking family. Instead, she's stuck here with my sorry ass." I scrub my hand over my face, feeling hopeless at this moment, not sure yet again if I have what it takes to make sure this amazing little girl has everything she needs.

"She has a family." He barks, looking at me like I have lost my damn mind.

"It's just me, man, look around. What family do you see?"

"You, me, Maddie, the twins, Pop. Hell, even Maddie's parents would love that precious little girl like she was their own. So, what if it is not a traditional family? It's still a fuckin family." I blow out a breath, hanging my head low.

"I didn't mean it like that. Trust me, I know you are all here for us. I just... hell, I don't know. I feel like I'm going to fail her. This is one thing in my life that I can't fail at." Shaking his head, he pats me on the back way harder than necessary.

"You won't fail her brother; you are going to be an amazing dad and just know we are all here to kick your ass if we see you messing up. That's what family is for." God knows I hope he's right.

"Dinners ready." We both look over to the back door as Maddie steps out, calling us for dinner. She looks beautiful today, glowing and genuinely happy, standing there rubbing her baby bump. Jealousy, jealousy is what I am feeling at this moment. Jealous that my best friend found something I never will. Jealous that everything has fallen into place for the both of them, even with all the bad shit life threw their way, they were able to overcome it. Still able to open themselves up to love one another, accept love, and create an amazing family together. All things I never thought I wanted, things I tried like hell to avoid until JoJo was dropped at my feet. Now I find myself jealous of shit that was never meant to be mine.

Dinner was fantastic. Maddie made homemade lasagna and garlic bread. It was delicious. But the best part was the company. We spent the night laughing and just being together, as a family. It's moments like these that I feel like everything will be okay, that JoJo can and will have a happy life here. At the end of the night, I have to pry her away from the twins so they can go home. If she's not in Sammie's arms being treated like a real-life doll, then she is following Seth around the house like a tiny shadow. She loves the twins, and I am so thankful to them both for showing her so much kindness and love. For playing with her even though they are older and no longer into the same things as her. It gives me hope we can make this crazy situation work for us. Perhaps I can give her the life she deserves.

Chapter 6

HARLEY

It is moving day. I'm not so sure this is a good idea anymore. There is no way this is going to work. We can't get along to save our lives and then there is JoJo. I know I'm going to love this little girl. I know I am going to get attached to her, and then what? Eventually, I'll have to move out. I can't stay forever and then he will eventually find someone, no matter what he says. They all do, and then I cannot be around anymore. I know if he was mine, I wouldn't want the nanny still coming around. No woman would, and I wouldn't be able to blame her for it. Would you want your man's old nanny hanging around his house, even though her services are no longer needed? No, I don't think so. So, then I lose another kid, only this time it's one I have formed a mom-like relationship with. One I have gotten to hold, love, and care for, like my own.

It would be hard on her as well. Although I'm sure she will get over it in time, I'm not so sure I could.

Harley, you handled it just fine with the twins. Yeah, but it's different with the twins. I still get to see them all the time. I can babysit whenever I want or just go hang out at their home anytime I want to because Maddie will always be my best friend. There will be no one who could stand between us and keep me away from them. No one to get jealous or to start any problems for us. So yeah, this is way different and much more complicated. A huge mistake. Of course, I can find the good in all this, that's why I choose to say yes in the first place. Yes, I need a place to live that was affordable, seeing how I could no longer afford to live in my home alone. It truly took Maddie and me both to pay all the bills. Yes, I am aware he needs help and wants it to be someone he can trust with his little girl. Lucky for me, that someone just happened to be me. However, he doesn't know how hard this is going to be on me. No one does. Barely anyone even knows I was married before, much less what all happened during that time in my life. The few people who do know I was married don't even know what happened. Just that we split up. Hell, even Maddie doesn't know, and you would think after she told me about all the crap she went through, I could tell her about mine.

My anxiety is through the roof. Perhaps Maddie can talk me down, or at the very least help me get my head on straight. She called and said she was on her way over now to help me declutter and split up the crap we accumulated after years of living together. I won't have the room for it all in one tiny bedroom, and the storage building I rented isn't big enough to hold all of this clutter. I have already moved all the things I know for sure are going into storage and have all the things I know for sure are going with me in the moving truck. Now I am pacing back and forth through the partially empty living room, in the house I have lived in for the past seven years, wondering why the actual fuck I'm even contemplating putting myself through this, knowing how it's going to end.

"What are you doing?" Maddie questions, as she walks through the front door. Stopping dead in my tracks, I quickly spin on my heels, clutching my chest.

"You scared the shit out of me. I didn't even hear you pull up." I say as I wrap my best friend in a big hug.

"What's wrong?" She asks, breaking the hug.

"I need to talk to you about something. Something I have been keeping secret for far too long." I huff out a breath and lead her into the kitchen where I have our old card table still set up. We always used it for outdoor crafts with the kids, and now it is set up as my makeshift kitchen table for the time being. She sits down across from me, rubbing her belly.

"Harley, you're worrying me. What's the matter? Why are you freaked out? I've never seen you so worked up like this." I drop my head into my hands.

"I don't even know where to start."

"Try with what you are worried about, or maybe from the beginning." She offers. I take a deep breath and decide to start at the beginning, then explain what is bothering me, so it makes more sense.

"You know how after high school, after you moved, I married Rhett, right?" She nods her head, waiting for me to continue. "Well, what you don't know is that shortly before we ran off to get married, I found out I was pregnant. That's why we got married so fast. He said his parents would be pissed if it got out that I was having his child and not married. That it would be a scandal and cause problems for their law firm." I glance up at her and can see the confusion on her face, seeing as I don't have a child. Before she can even ask, I continue.

"Well, two months into the pregnancy, I had gotten into a car accident. Remember, it wasn't bad, and everything looked fine with the baby as far as the doctors could tell. So, I was sent home with orders to rest. Seriously, I should have rested, but you know me. I can't sit still for long. I was up cleaning and moving things around in our new place, wanting nothing more than to make it a home. Within a few days, I started cramping badly, then the bleeding started and, well, long story short, I lost the baby." I can hear Maddie gasp from across the table. Looking up, I see the sadness and shock on her face.

"Oh my God, Harley, I'm so sorry. Why didn't you ever tell me?" I shrug my shoulders.

"No one even knew we were expecting except for the doctors and, well, Rhett. We wanted to wait awhile before we announced it. So, what was the point in telling anyone after the fact?" I shrug again, not having any other answer for her.

"Anyway, Rhett wasted no time in getting me pregnant again. In reality, it was way too soon and since my body didn't have the time, it needed to heal, and I hadn't gone back to the doctor to get checked after it was all said and done, well... I lost that one, too. After that, I went to the doctor to get checked out. They said it was because of all the scar tissue from the first miscarriage that they could do surgery to remove as much as they could, but there was no guarantee I would ever carry full term. Needless to say, Rhett wasn't happy about that. For him to get his hands on the money his parents had put in a trust for him, before he was thirty-five, he had to be married and have a child. If he met all of those stipulations, he would receive all the money at once and not in installments. I don't know the ins and out of the trust, but it had something about proving that he was mature enough or some bullshit like that to have access to that kind of money." Maddie laughs humorlessly.

"That's just plain stupid." I give her a sad smile.

"Yeah, tell me about it. So, after that, Rhett started pulling away from me. I didn't know it at the time, but he was pulling away from me because he was falling in love with his secretary. The one his parents hired for him when he graduated from law school and started working at their second office. He started coming home later and later every night until one night he didn't come home at all. Instead, I woke up the next morning to divorce papers being delivered to me and being told I had a month to find a new place to live. At least he was kind enough to transfer two thousand dollars into my bank account for a down payment." I glance back up at Maddie. I can see the fury in her eyes at how I was treated.

"Yeah, the best part, I found out not even a week after our divorce, that not only was he planning to marry Kimberly, his secretary, but she was pregnant. He was finally getting the kid he wanted so bad. Since I wasn't woman enough to do it, he had to find someone who was. His words, not mine." Maddie gets up, walks around the table, and wraps me in a much-needed hug.

"I'm so, so, so sorry, Harley. You didn't deserve to be treated that way. You deserve so much better than that. You are such an amazing person, and you couldn't help what happened."

"He didn't see it that way," I say in a cracked whisper. It's getting harder and harder to hold the tears at bay. "I'm not sad that he no longer wanted me. I could care less about that. We were never really in love with each other. The first pregnancy was a drunken accident. I'm sad because of what it left me. Not being able to be a mother myself, the one thing in life I always knew I wanted to be." She sits back down, grabbing my hands in hers.

"Did you ever have the surgery?" She asks, looking like she is about to cry herself.

"I did, but like I said, there's no guarantee it will work. My body might never be able to carry a baby full term." Rubbing my hand, she speaks softly, much like she does with the twins when she is trying to comfort them.

"But it could work. There's always a possibility that it

would." The first tear streaks down my cheek as I shake my head no.

"I don't want to take that chance. I don't think I could survive it again." We sit in silence for what seems like forever, neither of us knowing what to say next. Maddie breaks the silence.

"What made you decide to tell me about all of this? Not that I'm not glad that you trust me with something that is weighing so heavy on you, but why now? Why today?" I pull my hands out of hers, drying my face and taking a deep breath.

"I'm scared. I am scared I am going to get too attached to Jojo. Then, when I am no longer needed, and he has found someone to love, I will no longer get to be a part of her life. Here I will be again losing another child, and it might break what's left of my heart." She shakes her head.

"He wouldn't do that; he would never keep her away from you." I sigh.

"He might not plan to. He may say he never would, but that could all change if whoever he ends up with doesn't want me around. He would want to keep her happy, not me." I get up, heading back to my bedroom, needing a little space for a minute. A few minutes later, I hear Maddie come in. She is leaning against the door frame when I turn around, her arms crossed over her chest.

"You can change your mind, you know. He can find someone else. I can watch her until he does." I look down at my hands, picking at my nails like I do when I'm nervous.

"That's the fucked-up thing, though, Maddie. I know I can change my mind, but yet a part of me doesn't want to. Even knowing the heartache, I am most defiantly going to face, I don't want to miss the opportunity to be a part of her life. I don't want to miss the chance to feel what it's like to be a mom. Even though I know that's not the role I'm going to play, it's the closest I will ever get." I sniffle back more tears.

"Oh, Hunny." She says quickly, walking towards me, pulling me into her once again. "What can I do? How can I help to make all this easier for you?" She asks as she rubs a soothing hand over my back.

"I don't know. I think I just needed to get it all off my chest. I needed someone besides just Rhett and me to know."

"Well, you know no matter what, you can always talk to me about anything, Harley." As I pull away, I smile at her.

"I know. I'm sorry I took so long to tell you," I say to her as she smacks my arm gently.

"You stop with that right now. You told me when you were ready to talk about it." I knew she would understand. She always does. She knows better than anyone what it's like to have secrets you're not ready to share.

The rest of the day goes by smoothly. We separate all the décor we bought together throughout the years. Laughed at all the fun memories we made in the house and had a good cry as we did one last walk-through, before locking the doors for the last time. Now here I am, sitting in Jack's front yard while Xander has the moving truck backed up to the front door, ready to unload. I, well, I am frozen to my seat, unable to move. Yet again not sure if I can handle what I have gotten myself into. I hear knuckles rap against my window. I look over to see Jack standing there, wrapped in a jacket bracing against this unusually cold winter day.

"You ready to get everything moved in? The room is all cleared out for you." He says before cupping his hands in front of his face and blowing on them for warmth. Well, I guess this is it. No more stalling now. I turn the key over, open the door, then step out.

"As ready as I will ever be, I guess." I walk around to my trunk, where I decide it would be best to keep the glass-blown flowers and vase that belonged to my grandmother before she passed away. Jack notices me struggling with trying to grab them all carefully and offers a hand. I hand the bulk of them over to him, gently placing them into his outstretched arms.

"Please be careful with them. They are all I have left of my grandmother's." He smiles at me.

"I'll guard them with my life scoot..." He lets his words die on his lips. I haven't even moved anything in yet and he is already having trouble using my name, instead of all those infuriating names he always calls me. I slam the trunk closed, shaking my head at him.

"You ever going to get my name, right?" I ask, trying not to laugh at the pinched up worried expression on his face.

"Sorry, it's a habit. I'll do my best." I let the laugh slip past my lips and watch as his shoulders relax.

"Lead the way, Jackass," I say, holding my arm out, and gesturing towards the front porch. They positioned the trailer at the back of his property, which makes sense seeing as he is planning to build a house at the front of his property. It's a nice place though, only a couple of years old, and well maintained. It has a nice, covered porch off the front, big enough to hold two rocking chairs and some plants. I make a mental note for when it's mine, it would be a lovely place to sit and enjoy a good cup of coffee while listening to the birds sing. The inside is just as charming, sure it's small, but it's open and has a farmhouse feel to it. The inside is all rustic and the whitewash cabinets are beautiful. The floors look to be hardwood as far as I can see, other than the bedrooms, which are carpet, and the bathrooms, which are tile.

"Did you do all this yourself?" I ask as he shows me around.

"Do what?" He asks.

"The floors? I've never been in a trailer with hardwood and tile floors before." He shakes his head as he continues walking down the hall towards JoJo's room.

"No, I ordered it this way. I wanted it to be nice, even if it was just a mobile home. Something to be proud of, to call my own. Anyway, this is JoJo's room." He says as he opens the door completely and we see her spinning around with her doll in her hands, making her dress flap around her. "She's a princess if you couldn't tell." He says with a chuckle, and pure love shining in his eyes for the little girl he wasn't prepared for, that was just dropped into his life out of nowhere.

"I can see that," I say, laughing as I crouch down to her level. "Hi JoJo, it's good to see you again. Who is this?" I ask, pointing to her doll.

"Elsa," she says, holding her out for me to see.

"Oh, she pretty," I say, smiling at her.

"Thank you." She goes back to playing, forgetting we are even in the room.

"Ready to get everything in?" Jack asks from behind me.

"Yep," I say, walking past him and heading off to the moving truck. Within two hours, we have everything in, and the room is mostly put together. I still have a lot of unpacking to do, but that is a problem for tomorrow. Right now, all I want to do is crash. I am exhausted.

I WAKE UP TO THE SOUND OF LAUGHTER COMING FROM the kitchen. The twinkling sound of JoJo's laughter brings a smile to my face, as I wonder what has her so happy this early in the morning. I stretch, climb out of my bed, and shuffle to the bathroom to brush my teeth and wash my face. I forgot my clothes in my haste to get to the bathroom, so I have to head back to my room to get dressed for the day. Before I can make it back down the hall, I run into JoJo's tiny frame.

"Yay, you're up. Daddy, she up, we can eat now." She yells as she grabs my hand, dragging me down the hall to the kitchen.

"Woah, I need to get dressed first, Princess." I laugh, trying to slow her down.

"No, you don't my's in my nightgown still." She says, continuing to drag me behind her. I know I could stop her. I know I should. It's in the rules that I wrote to be completely dressed outside of our rooms. Something tells me the baggie t-shirt I sleep in won't cut it for being completely dressed in Jack's eyes. I can hear the sharp inhale of air he takes when his eyes land on me, see his nostrils flaring as his eyes track up my exposed legs. The heat in his eyes is making me tingle from head to toe. I give him a sheepish smile as I try to tug my shirt further down my legs. This is not a good start to our arrangement.

Chapter 7

JACK

Just my luck. The temptress would come to breakfast with those long, toned, tan legs of her on full display. She has to know what her body does to men, so that would insinuate she has done this on purpose. Just to get a rise out of me, push me, see if she can cause me to fuck up, and give her a reason to ditch me. Not happening, I need her here too badly, JoJo needs her here. I will ignore the desire coursing through my veins for her. I'll show her I can handle anything she throws my way, as I quickly advert my eyes, turning my back to JoJo and her. I fill the three plates with food and go to set them on the table.

"If you two would excuse me, I need to go get dressed." I hear Harley shuffle behind me as she goes to leave.

"You didn't seem to be worried about it before. Sit, eat

before your food goes cold." I quip as I sit the plates on the table, then head to the fridge to fix JoJo a glass of chocolate milk.

"I was just headed back from the bathroom to get dressed when she dragged me in here. I forgot to take clothes with me. This wasn't intentional." She huffs, drawing my attention back to her. She now has her arms crossed defiantly under her breast, pushing them up and pulling at the thin, almost translucent material, leaving her pert nipples on full display. My gaze slowly travels down the length of her body, noting her leg is popped out while she taps her toe on the floor in annoyance. Her annoyance doesn't bother me at the moment, not with the hem of her shirt now riding high up her beautiful thighs. It takes all my willpower not to drop to my knees in front of her and beg her to throw out the rules she insisted on. To give in to temptation, just once with me, and make sure she never regrets it. I can't do any of that though, so instead, I turn around and begin pouring us both a cup of coffee.

"You're good. Just sit down and eat." I grunt as I adjust my length in my sweats, hoping she doesn't notice the monster wants to come out to play. "How do you like your coffee?" Silently thanking God that I won't be able to see her legs anymore right now, as I hear her take a seat at the table.

"Cream and sugar, please," she replies. I nod my head before continuing my task. I place her cup in front of her before taking my seat across the table.

"What do you want to do today, JoJo?" I ask to break the awkward silence in the room.

"I know, I know, we go play with the kids!" She says with a mouth full of bacon and a hell of a lot of enthusiasm. It takes everything I have not to roll my eyes. She loves the twins and would spend every second of every day with them if she could.

"I will call Xan and see if they are free today. How does that sound?" She squeals her excitement, bouncing in her seat, eliciting a laugh from both Harley and me. The remainder of breakfast passes smoothly. Harley and JoJo keep chatting, trying to get to know each other, as I watch in amazement at how fantastic Harley truly is with kids. It's a wonder she doesn't have a few of her own. After I finish eating, I excuse myself from the table to clean up the mess I made while cooking. I wish I had waited, because shortly after I start washing dishes, Harley makes her way over to me, placing her dishes in the sink.

"Thank you for breakfast." She says quietly from my side. She's too close and in nothing but a t-shirt, or I assume there's nothing else under there. Could be wishful thinking on my part. It would be a lot easier to conceal the effects she has on my body if I were still sitting at the table. However, I'm not, so instead I move my hips in closer to the counter, hoping she doesn't see how fucking hard she makes me.

"You're," Wow, I wasn't expecting my voice to sound so husky, I have to clear my throat and try again. "You're welcome." Better, not much, but better. At least I sounded less like I was ready and willing to ravage her body all night long, which I am, but I won't be telling her that. No, I will hide the way she makes me feel. There are more important things to worry about, like getting the results from the DNA test later today, and making sure JoJo is happy and healthy. My depraved thoughts about this stunning woman are currently wreaking havoc on my libido, which will have to take a back seat for now and possibly forever. I cannot mess this up and think with my dick will surely cause problems for us all. He doesn't have the best track record so far at keeping us out of trouble. He is, however, surprisingly good at getting us into some of the best kinds of trouble. So, I can't really complain.

The paternity test results came back. JoJo is definitely my daughter. I wasn't prepared for how relieved I would feel from hearing that. I never wanted to be a dad until she showed up in my life. Now I couldn't imagine my life without her in it. We had just gotten to Xan and Maddie's house so JoJo could play with the twins when I got the phone call from Tammy. She's a friend from back in my time in foster care. She also happens to be a social worker herself now and promised to do all she could to ensure I obtained full custody of JoJo. She seems to believe that it won't be too difficult seeing as Brandy just left her with me, with absolutely no means of contacting her. I gave Tammy all the information I had on Brandy from before and copies of the notes that she left behind. Now Tammy is working endlessly to find her so she can hopefully sign over her rights without a fuss. That's what she said she wanted before she stormed out of my front door without a backward glance. I just pray she hasn't changed her mind. Not that I don't want JoJo to have a mom in her life, because I do. But if she was willing to abandon her like that, and if she's still doing the same things as before, then JoJo is better off without her. No kid should ever be deserted like that. If Brandy is still on Coke, which I bet she is, JoJo certainly doesn't need to be around the company she keeps. She's safer here with me. I just wish I had more to offer her than just me.

We are sitting outside watching the kids play, enjoying their laughter and relaxing.

"So, when are you gonna tell JoJo the good news?" Maddie questions, snuggling into Xan's side.

"I want to wait until we are sure she can stay with me. I don't want to get her hopes up." Maddie gives me a sad smile.

"That makes sense. Maybe we can plan a party or something to let her know when you find out for sure. That would be fun." She says with so much hope in her brown eyes, there is no way I can tell her no. Xan would most likely kill me if I broke her heart like that.

"Yeah, that sounds good Maddie, thank you for the idea. Would you like to help plan it?" Excitement spread across her face as she beams up at me.

"I would love to. How is everything going so far with Harley living with you?" I have to suppress a groan, shifting uncomfortably as images of her this morning flash through my mind.

"Fine," I grunt, causing Maddie and Xan to both stare at me quizzically.

" Are you two not getting along?" Xan asks with a raised brow. He knows we never get along.

"Nothing out of the ordinary," I reply, raking my hand through my hair. Xan is laughing, and Maddie is fighting not to join in. "Oh, you think it's funny, asshole?" Now Maddie is laughing too, and I can't help but join in.

"She can be a handful," Maddie says, wiping a tear from the corner of her eye.

"She's not so bad. She's great with JoJo and that's all that matters." I say shrugging my shoulders. In reality, we have been getting along fine, actually, we have spent little time together. My only problem is remembering to keep my greedy hands to myself. To try not to seduce her, or convince her of how amazing it would be for her to spend the night bouncing on my cock. Because as much fun as I know it would be, it could also cause more problems for us than we need at the moment.

IT'S BEEN TWO WEEKS SINCE HARLEY MOVED IN WITH US. There haven't been any more incidents with her being half-naked in my presence again. Not sure if I should be relieved about that fact or sad that I no longer get to see those legs of hers on display. I have gone back to work, so we barely see one another. She's gone to work by the time JoJo, and I are up and going, and in bed by the time I come in from work. Sunday is the only day we are at home at the same time. We still haven't heard a word from Brandy. It doesn't appear Tammy has had any luck finding her, either. She said two weeks and she would sign her over if I wanted to keep her, so why she hasn't shown back up is beyond me. You would think for someone who wanted her life without a kid attached so badly, she would dump them with someone they didn't know would be more than willing to be accessible to sign the needed paperwork. My head snaps up when I hear Xan entering the break room.

"Hey man, have you heard anything yet?" He asks as he pulls the lunch Maddie packed him from the fridge, taking a seat across the table from me.

"Nothing." I sigh, letting my head drop into my hands.

"Don't give up. You will have custody before you know it." He has more faith in the system than I do. He never lived in it. The bell chimes before I can respond, letting us know someone has come into the shop.

"I've got it. Finish your lunch, man," I say, standing from my spot, heading to the front.

"Welcome to Xan Ink. How can I help you?" I ask the lady standing at the sidewall, looking through the tattoo designs we have on display. She's cute, young but cute. She stands at maybe five feet and looks to be one hundred pounds soaking wet. With long multicolored hair of blue, pink, and purple. She's wearing all black, and fishnet stockings. At least I think that's what they are called. She turns around and I get the full effect of her ensemble. I almost laugh. I can't quite tell if she is trying to look older or tougher than she actually is.

"Umm... is Xander here?" She asks with her head bowed and shoulders up to her ear.

"He's taking a break, but I can help you?" I ask. She looks up and her icy blue eyes lock on mine. She pulls her shoulders back, standing taller, as determination settles into her.

"I don't need your help. I need to speak with Xander. It's important that I speak with him now." Now she has me intrigued. I have to know what this little thing could want with Xan.

"Give me a sec. I'll go get him." I say with a smirk before I turn on my heel heading back to the break room.

Xan is looking at his phone, typing away when I walk in.

"What?" Xan asks looking worried when I lean against the doorway with an amused smirk on my face.

"Oh nothing, there's just a cute little thing out there demanding to speak with you immediately." I am fighting back a laugh at the look on his face.

"Me?" He points to himself, looking between a mixture of panicked and frightened.

"Yep, that's what she said." I laugh. He's not amused as he stands up from the table, stalking towards the front of the shop.

"How can I help you?" He asks as politely... ish as he can, given he is worried about what she could possibly need with him specifically.

"Hi, my name is Hope, Hope Jones." She states, holding her

hand out for him to shake. He raises his brow, crossing his arms over his chest. She drops her hand back by her side. "Look, I don't know how to do this. I'm Bret's sister. I am so sorry for the pain he has caused. He hasn't been a part of my life since I was six, so I didn't know I had a niece and nephew until I saw what happened on the news, then went to the hearing. I have no other family left and would love to meet them, get to know them, and just be a part of their lives, no matter how small. If you think Maddie would be okay with it, I'd love to meet them." Well shit, I did not see that coming. Obviously, Xan didn't either, if the look of pure confusion on his face is any indication.

"She never mentioned Bret had a sister." She lets out a small, lackluster laugh.

"I have no doubt he never mentioned me to her. He hates me, I don't know why. He just always has." She shrugs her shoulders, looking sad at the thought of that despicable man, hating her. I would think after all he had done; she would hate him and not care what he thinks.

"Why did you come here instead of contacting Maddie directly?" I ask, since it doesn't appear that Xan is going to.

"I had no way of contacting her. Xander was easy to find." She tells me with another shoulder shrug.

"Leave your number with me. I'll pass it along to Maddie and if she chooses to meet with you, she will call." Xan offers, and I watch as the first smile she has given us crosses her face.

"Thank you so much," she says. Xan grunts as she writes

her number down on one of our business cards. It's not long before she is heading back out the door.

"You think that's a good idea?" Xan slips the number into his pocket.

"I don't know, man, but I can't keep it from Maddie." He lets out a long sigh, dragging his hands down his face. I pat his shoulder before heading back to the break room to call and tell JoJo good night.

Harley answers the phone right before it goes to voice mail, giggling and sounding out of breath. "Hello." She laughs out.

"What are you two up to?" I question, settling back into my chair.

"Just spinning in circles, getting dizzy and trying to stay standing." She giggles. I can see them stumbling all over the place, laughing their heads off, and it brings a smile to my face.

"Be careful. I don't want either of you getting hurt." I tell her, pulling the phone from my ear when I receive a text message. A picture of a smiling JoJo, her curly blonde hair, is stuck out in every direction. Face red from laughter, and all the spinning they were doing.

"I would never let her hurt herself." Harley huffs. Fuck, I've pissed her off, and that was not my intention.

"I know you wouldn't." I quickly tell her, hoping she will believe me. She's quiet for a moment. Then I hear her sigh.

"Here's JoJo." She says, completely ignoring my previous statement, brushing me off like always.

"Hey, Daddy." My little girl's happy voice rings through the line, making my smile grow wide across my face.

"Hey, Little Monster," I reply. She huffs, and I can picture her stomping her foot.

"My not monster, my princess daddy." I chuckle at all the sass wrapped up in such a tiny package.

"Alright Princess, are you having fun?" I can hear her shuffling around, no doubt settling into bed.

"Yep, Harley is the best." We talk for the next few minutes, her telling me all about her day until she yawns.

"Get some sleep Princess, good night." She let out another yawn.

"Good night daddy, I love you." My chest squeezes, and my heart swells a little more with pride at having such an amazing child.

"Love you too, baby girl," I say as I hang up the phone. I take a moment to think about how much joy Jojo has brought to my life in the little time she has been with me. I meant it when I said, I love her and now I can't imagine my life without her.

The rest of the night goes by quickly. We stayed busy with people coming in all night for new ink and piercings. Unfortunately, I got stuck with all the piercings. Normally it doesn't bother me, however, tonight it was a royal pain in my ass. One customer was Shannon Walker. This woman cannot seem to catch a hint, even if it smacked her in the face. I knew before I ever touched her, yet I still did. This is what happens when you think with your cock instead of your brain. Not only did I show her the time of her life, but I did it rapidly for two months straight, which I never do. I tried to let her down gently after JoJo showed up on my doorstep. I have no time to entertain Shannon, or any woman, for that matter. Tonight was no different. She refused to take no for an answer. Instead, she chose to keep trying to rub herself against me any chance she got. She originally came in just to have her new ink checked, but when she learned Xan was busy with a large back piece that would keep him tied up all night, she quickly decided she had to have her vertical clitoral hood pierced. What better time than tonight? I'm not entirely sure what she was thinking. Like flashing her cunt in my face and moaning anytime I had to touch her was going to change my mind. Not happening. I kept her around longer than I ever usually would, just out of pure laziness and convenience. I was about to ditch her clingy ass, anyway. By the time I make it home, I am exhausted, annoyed, and sex-deprived.

I was hoping the exhaustion would win out, but after two hours of tossing and turning in my bed, I gave up and headed to the kitchen for a bottle of water. I was not prepared for the sight I walk in on. Fuck me. Harley is bent over, grabbing a bottle of water from the bottom of the fridge. I was right the other day. She wears absolutely nothing under that thread bared shirt she sleeps in. Her position leaves no room for imagination. Every magnificent inch of her little cunt and round ass is on display for my greedy eyes. A loud groan leaves my chest. She snaps up, pulling her shirt down, covering her perfection from view. I am adjusting my length in my gray sweats as she spins on me, the action drawing her gaze. I watch her tongue peek out, sliding across her full bottom lip as she takes in the magnitude of the monster hidden in my pants. The lust in her eyes does nothing to help curb my desire for her. All I can think about is dragging her to my bed and having my filthy way with her all night long.

Chapter 8

HARLEY

I sense his presence before I hear his sharp intake of air. Fuck my life. Before I went in search of a bottle of water, I should have put on some clothes. I almost turned back five times during my short walk from my room to the kitchen, but I told myself he would be asleep, so why waste my time? I should have known better. It is just my luck he would catch me bent over in the fridge, with all my goodies on display. I hate him. It is his fault I am in here looking for something to cool me off, anyway. He is the one that made a sexy as hell appearance in my dreams, leaving me all hot and bothered. Now, I am in here breaking one of my own rules instead of being in bed asleep. I snap up, turning to face him, my gaze snagging on his hand, which is currently adjusting an impressively large bulge in his gray sweats. Why, why do all the hot guys know to dress in gray sweats? Is that a class they teach in high school? Quickly, I avert my eyes. That view is not helping the situation. I am almost certain I am drooling now. Not only can I see the magnitude of what he is working with, but he is also shirtless, and his sweats hang so low on his waist they are mere inches away from showing me all he has. That impressive V of his is begging me to trail my tongue over it. *Stop Harls, you know better,* I mentally berate myself.

"The fuck Shadow?" He growls out, causing a shiver to race down my spine. I. Fucking. Hate. This. Man.

"How was I to know you were going to come in here?" I snap back, cocking my hip out and crossing my arms over my chest. Watching his eyes heat as they take me in from head to toe.

"You're a fucking prick tease. You know that?" He says with a smirk on his face. I cannot tell if that bothers him or if it excites him in some fucked up way. Possibly a combination of the two.

"Again, there was no way for me to know you would walk in here. Sorry, but that does not make me a tease. Just extremely unlucky." The longer he drinks me in, the more annoyed I become. I have never wanted to climb a man like I do this one, yet I hate him and that trumps the unwanted desires coursing through my veins. I really should consider investing in a robe.

"You know exactly what you are doing, Shadow. Don't play with me. It gives you a thrill. You know it does." I roll my eyes in a huff.

"Whatever Jackass." I push my way past him, only to have

him grip my waist, pulling me back against him. His length nuzzling snuggly against my ass has me fighting to suppress a moan.

"If you crave my monster cock, baby girl," He purrs in my ear, grinding against me. "All you have to do is ask. I would be more than happy to oblige." A sound that could only be described as a mixture of a growl and a moan leaves my throat. My head is spinning at his closeness. The feel of him against me, his woodsy, masculine smell assaulting my senses, is overwhelming me. Moments like this, it is hard to remember why I loathe this man so much.

Finally, breaking the spell, he had me under, I pull away from him.

"You wish I wanted to play with that little thing, but I have better things to do with my time." I throw over my shoulder, as I quickly head back to my room. He is laughing by the time I close my door behind me, leaning against it to catch my breath and hopefully regain control over my raging libido. No doubt he knew how turned on I was by him. Will I ever admit it to him? Hell fucking no. Can I admit it to myself? Occasionally, like now when I am so worked up that I am literally dripping wet, in need of a release. I move over to my bedside table, reaching into the top drawer, fully intending to put my vibrator to good use.

"If you really want to play this game, Harley, we can play." He rasps out from the other side of my door. Fuck, there goes my plan. No way I am giving him the satisfaction of hearing me pleasure myself, especially when he is the star in my dirty fantasy. I let out a heavy sigh, closing the drawer back and climbing back under my covers. Rubbing my legs together, trying to ease the ache. I toss and turn for hours before I fall back to sleep, dreaming of all the sinfully delicious things I would love to do to Jack and his huge package.

I AM IN A FOUL MOOD THIS MORNING. NOT ONLY DID I GO to bed needy and wanton, but I also woke up the same fucking way with no release in sight. I have to go to work, then come home and watch JoJo. I will have no time for myself or my needs until this weekend. Thankfully, this weekend I am off, and I know just who to call. Drake Nelson, my friend with benefits, my always on-call, booty call. Well, as long as he is single, that is. I will have to check on that. I have not called on him in a while. Actually, the last time I had seen him was the night Maddie had a meal with Xan at Pop's bar. Not that I called on him that night, I just ran into him. He and the girl he had been seeing had broken up, she cheated on him, and he needed some cheering up. I had planned on catching up with him the next day since our night had been interrupted, but work took him out of town, and we have not spoken since. I shoot him a quick text before I get dressed for the day.

> Me: Hey D, how's it hanging?

I giggle to myself as I sit my phone down to dig my clean scrubs out of the laundry basket on my closet floor. I did not feel like putting them away last night. Now I get to walk around in wrinkly scrubs all day, great. I have got to stop doing this. It takes a whole five minutes out of my life to put them away. I would never leave my dresses in a basket all night like this. In no time, I am dressed, ready for the day, and prepared to quietly sneak out of the house. I refuse to deal with Jackass this morning. As I enter the kitchen, looking down at my phone, I head straight for my coffee in the fridge. I don't want to hang around waiting for the coffee to perk. Besides, I love cold coffee and I can grab breakfast on the way to work. I look up just in time to see it coming, but not fast enough to stop it. One minute I am scrolling Facebook, the next I face planting Jack's bare chest. And what a magnificent chest it is. Everything about this man, physically, that is, is sinfully magnificent.

His arms and chest both are covered in tattoos, packed with muscles, wide shoulders, a defined six-pack that tappers into a delicious V that dips into his low-slung and snug-fitting gray sweatpants. The same fucking pants he was tempting me in last night. Have mercy, there is no way I am going to survive this. He really is a sexy male specimen. His hair has grown a good bit this past year, he still wears it brushed back and cut close on the sides. His beard is longer as well and happens to make his already sexy face look even better. It seriously would make the perfect seat. His stomach is the only visible part of his body not covered in tattoos. I know he has them on his back and calves, from the fourth of July party last year at Xan's house. He grabs my shoulders, pushing me back from him gently, studying me with a smirk on his face.

'Whoa there, Shadow." He says, trying his best not to laugh. Why does God hate me? What did I ever do to deserve this type of cruel and unusual punishment? I refuse to meet his stare, but staring at his arms isn't much better. Have you ever heard of arm porn? It's a thing and I am almost positive it was created just for his arms. All the corded muscles and bulging veins will make even a nun's mouth water.

"Sorry, I didn't see you there," I mutter, shaking out of his hold and stumbling to the fridge. After grabbing my coffee, I head out.

I have one foot out the front door when Jack speaks again.

"What's the rush, Harley?" He asks, coming up behind me, standing extremely too close.

"I umm... nothing, I just have some, ahh, things I need to do before work. That's all." I stammer out, trying to keep my shoulders back and my eyes facing forward. *Do not look at him, Harley, no good can come from it. He knows what he is doing. He said it last night, he is just playing the game. Trying to see how far he can push me, bend me before I break. Giving in to my desires and handing myself over to him. Not happening, I refuse to be another notch on this man's bedpost.* Stepping in so close his chest presses into my back, he grips my hips, brings his lips so close to my neck I can feel the whisper of the connection when he murmurs.

"Have a good day beautiful, I will see you when you get home." God help me, he is playing dirty.

"Umm... Yeah, o-okay." I manage to squeak out. I feel his lips pull into a smile against my flesh before he places a feather-light kiss on my pulse point. He knows what he is doing to me, how much his nearness, his touch, his lips, hell, even his words affect me. He is purposely wreaking havoc on my body.

"I have to go." I breathe out, sounding wonton and needy even to my ears. With jerky movements, I break his hold and make my way to my car. I need that time out and away from him now more than ever. My head is swimming with a mix of emotions the entire way to work. Lust, annoyance, need, hatred, amusement, frustration, any emotions someone could invoke in another person, whirling around in me, crashing into one another, fighting for the first-place position. I am so focused on all these feelings; I damn near pass the turn to the parking lot of Rose Grove family health. Before Jack finds a way to ruin my day, I need to shake him from my mind.

I am still a pent-up bundle of sexual tension by the end of my workday, and I still have not heard back from Drake yet. Looks like this will be a dull weekend out after all. I wonder if I can talk Becky into going out with me if she's not working. I let out a huff of frustration when I pull up in front of Jack's. Letting my head fall back against the seat, I take a few deep breaths to prepare myself for whatever he has in store for me this afternoon. Inhaling through my nose, exhaling out of my mouth, in, out, in, and out again. *You can do this, Hurley. Being a bitch to him, and brushing off his advances, has never been a problem before now. There is no reason for it to be one now.* Except I know that is not true. Before, I was sure he was flirting just to annoy me. Now, I know he seriously wants me, and I just cannot give into him. It would cause too many problems, which would definitely fuck up everything. It would make things hella awkward when we are forced to be at Maddie and Xander's events. Parties, Christmas, their wedding, hell, the birth of their child. I try imagining how fucking weird it would be to be stuck in a hospital room in such proximity to Jack while meeting the newest addition to the family. If I gave in to this pull and everything crashed and burned around us, like I have no doubt it will, everything would be ruined. I reluctantly exit my car and head inside, might as well get this over with. The sooner I go in, the sooner he leaves for work, and the less I have to see him. The rest of my night will be peaceful. I am taken aback when I walk in and see that dinner is already cooked and on the table. He never cooks dinner before he leaves. I always cook after I get home. He usually takes leftovers from the night before to the shop with him. It has been our routine since I moved in. So, why the change today?

"Waterpipe busted at the shop, so we decided to close today. Xan has some guys from Smith's Complete Construction coming out to fix it. You can have the night off if you would like, or you can stay and have dinner with us. I have made plenty of food." I force a polite smile onto my face.

"Thank you, but I think I will head out for the night if you will be home," I say, heading to my room to change clothes. I send Drake another text. I hate seeming needy, but I really hate going out alone.

> Me: D, you up to meet at Pop's for a few drinks?

He finally texts back as I'm walking back out of my room.

> D: Can't, out of town again. Maybe next time.

I try Becky next. Hoping with any luck, she will be free to hang out tonight.

> Me: Becky, you up for drinks at Pop's?

> Becky: Working, but it's not busy and I only work a half shift tonight. If you're okay to wait for me to get off, I'm down.

Thank God, waiting is better than nothing.

> Me: Sounds good to me, headed your way now.

With that I tell JoJo bye, ignoring Jack, and head out the door. With any luck, he will be fast asleep when I get home.

In no time at all, I make it to Pop's. I have already had two shots by the time Becky climbs on the barstool next to me.

"What's up chicka? What caused this spur of the moment

'let's get wasted' night?" She asks, bumping her shoulder into mine. I look over at her. She is beautiful, I don't understand how Justin ever let her go. She is a little shorter than me, with long, curly, red hair, a light splattering of freckles across her nose and cheeks, and bright green eyes with flecks of gold mixed in. If she wasn't such a good friend, I might scoop her up for myself. Joking, partially, but seriously, I probably would if I didn't like cock so much. I know Justin and Becky are meant for one another, even if they haven't quite realized that for themselves just yet, they will one day. In the meantime, she is now my only single girlfriend to hit the town and get wasted with, when I need to wipe one Jackson Xavier Williams out of my head.

"Just needed some girl time," I reply as I tip my next shot of whiskey back, downing it in one go without even wincing. She doesn't argue, doesn't ask more questions, or pry into what is bothering me. Instead, she holds up two fingers to Bob, requesting more shots. We spend the next few hours drinking way more than either of us needs. More than the legal limit, that is for sure. I call Maddie for a ride home. Bob took our keys, refusing to let either of us leave on our own.

"Talk." Xander quips, answering Maddie's phone. I look down at the screen to be sure I called the right number. I did.

"Hey Xan, we need a lift home." I slur out, giggling.

"I can't tonight, and neither can Maddie. She has been sick all day. Morning sickness has been kicking her ass lately. I can call Jack." I can hear him rustling around on the other end.

"No, he doesn't need to get JoJo out this late." I blurt out.

"Fuck, you're right. I'll call Justin. I'm sure he will pick you up. Wait, who is 'we'?" He asks just now realizing I told him, *'We need a lift,'* to start with.

"Becky and me," I answer, rolling my eyes, then immediately regretting it when the bar starts spinning.

"I will just leave her name out when I ask." He grunts. Asshole.

We are stumbling out of the bar for fresh air when Justin pulls into the lot. Xan sent me a text, so I knew Justin was coming. Becky, however, did not. I may have forgotten to mention it to her. I realize this when she stiffens next to me, stopping dead in her tracks. Justin is going to be pissed and because I am drunk, I will most likely laugh.

"Mother fucker." Becky mutters from my side. I should have told her, I know, but it slipped my mind in my drunken state. Justin's expression doesn't seem much better when he hops down from his truck.

"Come on, then." He grunts, gesturing to his truck. I stumble my way over, dragging Becky behind me. She's shaking her head no while holding her hands over her face.

"Come on, I will make him drop you off first," I say, hoping it helps ease her worries.

"No can do." He grumbles, lifting us one at a time, placing us in the truck, her in the middle seat closest to him. "You are closest to the bar. Becky's parents live down the road from me. No way am I am going to backtrack this time of night. I will drop you off at Jacks, then take her home." He closes the door on us before I could respond. The ride to Jack's is filled with silence, and Becky has pressed herself against me, trying to put as much distance between her and Justin as she can. I hate to leave her alone with him, but I know there is no changing Justin's mind once it is made up.

"Text me later," I whisper to Becky before Justin can make it around to help me down. She nods her agreement, sliding over to my seat and wrapping her arms around herself. I stumble my way to the door, fumbling with my keys for what felt like a solid five minutes. Since Justin had just pulled onto the road, it couldn't have been. I make my way through the door, almost face planting the floor a few times, causing me to giggle. That is until my eyes land on Jack. He is leaning against the wall, blocking my way down the hall to my room. Arms crossed over his chest; he looks extremely pissed at my current state. That makes no sense, I was off for the night, not home with JoJo. I can do whatever the fuck I want in my free time, damn it.

"Seriously Scooter." He says, shaking his head in disappointment.

"Seriously Jackass." I cross my arms, trying to look just as annoyed as he does. Obviously, I fail, if Jack's expression is any indicator. His gorgeous mouth slowly lifts in a smile. Fuck him.

Jack swaggers over to me when I start to sway on my feet. I don't need his help, dammit. This isn't the first time I have been stumbling drunk, and I'm sure it won't be the last.

"Let's get you to bed, Huffy." He smirks, wrapping his arm

around my waist, and starts to lead me to my room. I want to complain that he is breaking the rules using those infuriating nicknames, but I worry he will let me go, and being in his arms feels too good. So, I bite back my snarky comment, leaning further into him. I'm drunk, I can always blame it on the alcohol later. He walks me to my bed, helping me to sit down.

"Stay." He demands, pointing a finger at me, then heads to my dresser and grabs my nightshirt off the top of it. "You need help?" He asks when he holds it out to me.

"Can you just unzip me?" I ask under my breath; I hate even asking, but I'd fall over if I tried to do it myself right now. He nods his head. I stand, turning slowly, hoping the room doesn't spin any faster than it already is. My breath catches in my throat at the feel of his knuckle brushing against my spine as he lowers my zipper. Holding the front of my strapless dress so it doesn't fall, I turn back to face him.

"Thank..." I sway again before I can finish thanking him for all he has done to help. He guides me back to my bed, sitting me down as he pulls the shirt over my head.

"Arms in." He grunts, holding the shirt still so I can ring my arms through the armholes. Kneeling in front of me, he gently removes my shoes, placing them under the edge of my bed, out of my walking path. "Come on, up." He pulls me to my feet again, adjusting my shirt so it covers me completely. "Now, do that lady magic and wiggle the dress off." He says, stepping back from me. I snort out a laugh.

"Lady magic?" I laugh harder.

"Yes smartass, you know... taking clothes off from under more clothes. I know you can all do it." Still laughing hysterically, I shimmy my dress off. Kicking it to the side, I lose my balance. Jack moves quick, wrapping his arms around me, pulling me flush with his body.

"You good?" I peer up at him, blinking a few times. I've lost my ever-loving fucking mind, because I start to lift myself, bringing my mouth closer to his. Before our lips connect, he turns his head, giving me his cheek. Embarrassed and slightly pissed, I try pulling away from him, but he refuses to release his hold on me.

"Not tonight, darling, not when you're drunk." His murmur against my forehead then places a feather-light kiss. "Alright, in you go." He pulls the covers back, helps me in bed, then tucks me in, placing another light kiss on my head. Where is this man any other time? I must be dreaming. That's all I can come up with. No way any of this is real.

Chapter 9

JACK

It has been two months since Harley moved in with us. Two months, two freaking long ass months that we have been playing the strangest game of striptease I have ever witnessed. I shit you not, that is the best way to explain whatever the fuck is going on in my house right now. I come home from work almost every night to find her moseying around the house in some kind of barely-there mesh getup, which leaves nothing for the imagination, not that I'm complaining. She is sexy as hell. It sucks I only get to look and not touch. It's torture, truly the worst kind of torture. She's playing dirty and I have no problem playing dirty myself. I may have started it, walking out in a pair of briefs and nothing else. I couldn't help myself after seeing her bent over in the fridge, then her trying to kiss me when she came home drunk. It took all my strength to turn away from her, but I refused to have her say the kiss was a drunken mistake. Hell, we didn't even kiss, and she still tried to say that. I know better. She does one hell of a job at hiding her interest in me, but I still see it when she thinks I'm not watching. I am always watching her. She demands my attention even though she doesn't want it.

The only time I have come home in the past two months and her not be almost naked was three days ago. Maddie wasn't feeling well, and we had no one at the shop, so we closed early. She wasn't expecting me home, and she was bundled up on the couch, watching some home improvement show. The surprise on her face was priceless. I already knew it was all just for show, just to get a rise out of me. More accurately, to make my cock rise. She sure as fuck doesn't walk around dressed like that in front of JoJo. She has been fully dressed or in her room ever since I called her on the game. Tonight, though, tonight is different. She's not hiding in her room; she's not walking around half-dressed either. No, she is in my shower. I came home to a note saying their shower was spraying funny, so she was using mine. She obviously loosened the showerhead. All I had to do was tighten it and it was spraying perfectly. I have no clue what the game is here tonight. Is she hoping I will walk in? Is she just trying to annoy me by holding up my bathroom when she knows I will want a shower and to get in bed? She's getting both.

I don't bother knocking. Slinging the door open, I stalk in and prop up against the sink, with my arms crossed over my chest. Watching her as the soap and water glide down her sexy as sin body.

"Nice." I have to bite back a laugh when she jumps at the sound of my voice.

"The fuck Jackass?" She huffs, copying my stance in the shower. She is mouth-wateringly beautiful, standing there all pissed, with water running down her amazingly curvy body. I watch as her tits rise and fall with each breath.

"You gonna try to pretend this isn't all part of your little strip tease game you've been playing?" I ask, raising a brow at her.

"No asshole, this is me trying to get a shower without ruining the other bathroom." She rolls her eyes, throwing her arm in the air.

"The shower head was loose; you could have easily fixed that." She lets out an annoyed little huff.

"How was I supposed to know that?" I shrug my shoulder, taking a step towards the shower. I love how she's not shy in the slightest. Her beautiful body is completely bare to me and yet she has done nothing to hide it. It's refreshing.

"I assumed you loosened it yourself," I state, pulling my shirt over my head.

"Why would I do that?" She shoots back without hesitation.

"To up this little game of yours?" I toss back, toeing my shoes off before unbuttoning my jeans. I watch her greedy little eyes drink me in as I lower my pants and briefs down my legs, my already hardening cock springing free from its restraints to point right at her. She licks her lips, her eyes darkening with lust.

"What are you doing?" She asks, her voice all breathy and wanton.

"Getting a shower so I can get in bed. Are you moving over or getting out?" She doesn't answer me, instead just stepping aside, letting me in under the spray.

"Now what?" She questions with her back pressed against the wall.

"Now I shower, then go to bed," I say back flatly, trying to conceal my smirk. She is starting to look a little nervous now. "I will not touch you, Harley, until you tell me that's what you want. I might be an asshole, but I would never force myself on a woman." She lets out a sigh, moving closer, her face finally softening a bit.

"I know you would never do that, Jack," she says, gently placing her hand on my cheek. I lean into her touch, closing my eyes and enjoying the feeling of her warm hand on my skin. "I might not like you, but I know you would never force yourself on someone." I chuckle, grabbing her hips, needing to feel her, but not wanting to push her too far. Leaning into her, so my lip grazes the shell of her ear with each word I murmur.

"Yet you're this close to me, naked and wet in my shower, just begging to be fucked. That doesn't seem like something someone who doesn't like me would do." She moves in closer, winding her arms behind my neck, tangling her fingers in my hair.

"Well, my usual friend with benefits is out of town. Desperate times call for desperate measures." Damn. This. Girl. That remark has me caught somewhere between a jealous rage and horny as fuck. The thought of someone else touching her shouldn't bother me like it does. I force the thought out of my mind, choosing to focus on this moment, this perfect little gift standing wrapped in my arms.

"Just say the word beautiful." She smirks and I watch as amusement dances in her eyes before she replies.

"The word." She is such a brat. I smack her ass, eliciting a squeal from her, before snatching her up and throwing her over my shoulder. I shut off the water before stalking out of the shower.

"Hey, I still need to wash my hair." She laughs, swatting at my back as I make my way into my bedroom.

"Fuck now, shower later," I growl, smacking her perfect little ass again, thoroughly enjoying the little mewling sounds she makes when I do so. When I reach the bed, I drop her onto it, following her down, so my body has hers pinned to the bed. "Are you sure about this? I don't want there to be any misunderstandings between us." I ask, peering down at her with my arms braced on either side of her head. She nips at my bottom lip.

"Positive." She murmurs against my mouth.

I break the kiss too soon, needing to be absolutely sure before we do anything more.

"No regrets, Harley," I mumble, kissing across her jaw and

down her long, slender neck. She hums her agreement, raking her nails down my back.

"Fuck me already Jack." She whimpers in my ear, grinding her core up against my stiff cock. I smile against her neck, loving the feeling of her squirming under me. She feels so perfect pressed against me.

"What's the rush, baby girl?" She growls, digging her fingertips into my ass, trying her damnedest to pull me closer, to get the friction she needs, that I'm denying her. Shaking my head, I grab her hands one at a time, pinning them above her head.

"If you're not going to fuck me Jackass, I can take care of myself." She seethes behind clenched teeth.

"Oh, I'm going to fuck you, angry girl. Patience." She huffs but stops, trying to wiggle out from under me. I continue kissing along her jaw, while I wrap her wrist in one hand, I trail the other down the length of her amazing body, reveling at how soft her skin is under my callused hands. Her breath catches in her throat when my fingers brush against her slit, sliding easily through her juices. She's so fucking wet and ready for me already. Using two fingers, I spread her lips, pressing my thumb to her clit, I rub in small tight circles as I suck her taut nipple into my hot mouth. Her moans begin to get louder, echoing through the room. I let her nipple go with a pop. Then crash my mouth down on hers. I stifle her cries of pleasure with a rough, demanding kiss.

"Be a good girl and keep quiet. We don't want to wake JoJo." I mumble against her mouth as I slip a finger inside her wet heat. She lifts her face to my shoulder, biting down into my flesh, pulling a guttural moan from my throat. Fuuuck... She is driving me insane. I need to be inside her now. I wanted to take my time with her, taste all of her, and give her so many orgasms she wouldn't even remember her name. That will all have to take a backseat for now. Right now, I just need to feel her wrapped completely around me. Reaching over to the nightstand, I dig around blindly for the strip of condoms I know are in there. When my fingers finally curl around the pack, I waste no time snatching it out, tearing it open, and rolling the rubber down my thick shaft. Fisting my cock in one hand, I line up with her tight little hole.

"You sure? Last chance to back out." She hooks her feet behind my ass, locking them together, trying to pull me into her.

"I'm sure." I need no more encouragement. I sink into her to the hilt in one powerful thrust.

"FUUUCK, baby, you feel so damn good," I grunt, pulling out to the tip and slamming back in again. She's so beautiful, with her head thrown back, her mouth hanging open as soft moans ring out around us, her eyes are shut, with a look of pure bliss on her face. The bite of her nails on my back makes me pound into her harder, both of us chasing our release, needing it like our next breath. At this moment, we aren't two people who can't seem to get along for the life of them. We are one, completely in sync with each other. Our dislike for one another is no match for our carnal needs and lust.

"So close." She pants, matching me thrust for thrust. Lifting one of her legs, I hook it over my shoulder, so I hit even deeper.

"Let go, baby, cum on my cock, let me feel your tight little pussy milk me dry," I growl. Thank fuck she's a good little girl and listens because I don't know how much longer I could hold off. She buries her face into the crook of my neck as she screams out her release, and I follow her into euphoric bliss. I collapse beside her, panting for air, trying to slow my racing heart. As soon as I have some of my bearings back, I head to the bathroom, trash the condom, and clean myself up. Grabbing a fresh washcloth, I wet it with warm water before heading back to the room to clean Harley up. She hasn't moved a muscle, still sprawled out like a starfish in the middle of my king-size bed, looking completely sated. Slowly, I crawl up between her spread legs, placing soft kisses along my way. When I reach her mound, I gently clean her before tossing the rag to the floor, placing a soft kiss on her tender flesh, and making my way up her delicious body. Settling back beside her, I pull her into my arms and pull the covers over our naked bodies, more than ready to call it a night.

"Sweet dreams, Princess," I murmur, planting a soft kiss below her ear. I'm almost asleep when I feel her pulling out of my arms, preparing to sneak out of my bed. "Where are you going, Princess?" I ask, tightening my hold around her waist.

"Umm, my bed. I... I think it would... no, I know it would be best for me to go back to my bed." She says as she untangles for me and climbs to her feet.

"I can make sure you're up before JoJo wakes up. Come back to bed." She ignores me, walking to the bathroom. When she comes back out, she is dressed for bed and has her dirty clothes and all of her fruity-smelling soaps in her arms.

"It's better that we don't share a bed Jack, best not to confuse this for more than it is." She says, walking to the door, not even glancing my way.

"And what would this be?" I ask, sitting up on the side of the bed, not bothering to cover myself back up.

"Fucking." She answers flatly, glancing over her shoulders at me. She quickly averts her eyes when she notices I am not remotely covered.

"Fucking?" I repeat. It sounds more like a question than a statement.

"Yes Jack, fucking, friends with benefits, or more like acquaintances with benefits in this case." She walks out the door, closing it quietly behind her. Well fuck, that just happened. I don't think I have ever had a woman friend zone me before, especially right after sex.

She's avoiding me. She's gone before I get up in the morning and when she gets home, she goes straight to her room.

"Harley," I call, knocking lightly on her door. She doesn't respond at first and I begin to worry that something more is wrong. I knock a little harder. She flings the door open with a scowl firmly planted on her face.

"What?" She huffs with her arms crossed and her hip jutted out. She is so fucking adorable when she is pissed, she always has been. I lean against the door frame, smirking down at her. "Do you need a wet wipe to clean that smirk off of my seat... I mean, your face?" She raises a brow at me. Her lips twitch as she tries to hold back her laughter at her comment. I, however, can't hold back my laugh.

"Your seat?" I ask, reaching out and pulling her flush with me.

"Shut it Jackass." She laughs, swatting at my chest.

"You've been avoiding me. Why? No regrets, remember." She sighs, pulling away from me.

"I'm not avoiding you. I just had... things... I needed to do is all." She stutters out. I can tell she was trying to come up with an excuse, but she couldn't think of anything.

"Oh, you had things to do, yeah. What kind of things?" She huffs, looking all kinds of pissed off.

"It's none of your business. I don't answer to you or any other man, Jack. Don't get confused thinking just because you got in my pants once means you own me." She pushes past me, heading to the kitchen. I follow close behind.

"I never said I owned you, Princess." What the hell is her deal today?

Chapter 10

HARLEY

I spin on Jack with my arms crossed over my chest, raising a brow at him.

"So, what's with the fifth degree, then?" He moves toward me, backing me up to the counter. He places his hands on either side of me, completely crowding my personal space.

"No fifth-degree Princess, just wondering why you spent the entire week avoiding me after you said there would be no regrets." I place my hands on his chest to push him away. That was a bad idea. He feels just as good under my palms today as he did last week.

"We can't do this; it was and needs to stay just a one-night thing. We gave in to our desires and do not need to make that mistake again." I sound breathy and needy even to my ears. *What the fuck, Harley? Get it together. This is not the first insanely attractive man you have had pressed against you, and it won't be the last.*

"We are most definitely doing that again, love, and a lot." He whispers with his lips brushing against my ear. A shiver rushes down my spine and my knees try to give out on me. What is this man doing to me? No one ever affects me like this.

"N-no Jack, really, I think we shouldn't. It will get too weird and could be horrible with us living together, especially for JoJo. We need to forget about last week, act like it never happened." He obviously isn't listing to me as he trails kisses down my neck.

"I think it would be perfect, all the benefits of a relationship without the relationship. JoJo won't know anything. We have time while she's asleep, take care of each other's needs, then go to our separate rooms." Is he suggesting a friend with benefits situation with his live-in nanny right now? This can't be happening.

"Friends with benefits? But we aren't even friends." I say, leaning my head to the side, giving him better access to my neck. I am obviously gluten for punishment. He makes me weak, even though I should be resisting him. *This is not good, not good at all.*

"We're friendly.... That's close enough to friends." He says, smirking down at me. I can't help but laugh at him.

"We are not friendly in the slightest," I tell him, still laughing.

"I think we were pretty friendly last week." He tells me.

"No... we were horny last week." I reply.

"Horny, friendly. What's the difference?" He asks, wrapping my hair around his fist and pulling my head back so I'm looking up at him. "I say we add to that little contract of yours. I don't have the time to go out chasing tail now, so I say we use each other to take care of our needs. No strings attached, just some fun. You don't do serious, I don't do serious, it's perfect. We don't have to worry about anyone catching unwanted feelings or wanting something we aren't prepared to give. Just a lot of fantastic orgasms." He says all of this as he trails his hand up my inner thigh, then cupping my already drenched pussy through my leggings. "You know you like the sound of that. You're soaked just thinking about it." God, I hate this man.

"JoJo could walk in here any minute Jack; you need to stop," I tell him but do nothing to stop him as he slips his hand into my pants, dipping his fingers between my folds, rubbing delicious circles on my swollen nub.

"So wet." He groans into my shoulder. "She's not here, she went with Maddie, Xan, and the twins to get ice cream." He dips a finger into my pussy, and I about come undone on the spot. "Come on, sweetheart, just say yes. You know you want to. You know I won't disappoint." He stops all movement but doesn't remove his fingers from inside of me. I need the release he is denying me, and I find myself riding his hand. He chuckles, shaking his head at me.

"Tisk, Tisk Princess. If you want to cum, you know what you have to do. Just give in and agree." He pulls his hand back, sucking my juices from his fingers. His moan at the taste of me is almost enough to make me cum.

"Fine, say I agree with this nonsense. What are the rules? We have to have rules so that it doesn't come back to bite us in the long run." I try to sound less affected by him than I am, but know I am failing miserably.

"I'd be happy to bite you." He smirks. "As for rules... it's simple, if you need an orgasm, you come to me, no one else. I don't share and have no desire to catch anything. If you're not on birth control, get on it. I hate condoms. No getting attached or falling in love. I don't have time for bullshit." He shrugs his shoulder. "So, what do you say?" I cock my head to the side.

"I don't want to catch shit either, asshole, so you can't be going around poking your dick into every wet hole you find either." Apparently, he takes this as an agreement because before I know what's happening, I am slung over his shoulder, and he is stalking towards his room.

"The only hole I'll be poking my dick in is yours." He says, smacking my ass before throwing me down on the bed. "Birth control?" He asks as he yanks my shirt over my head.

"Pill." Is my only answer before his mouth crashes down on mine. His kiss is toe-curling hot. He slides his tongue into my mouth, massaging his tongue against mine while grinding his hard cock into my core. "Please," I whine, lifting my hips, begging for more.

"Is that a yes, Princess?" This smug bastard. I should say no, if for any other reason than just to prove he can't always get his way, but I need this. D has been out of town for a while now, so I can't call him for a release.

"Fine... yes," I answer with a huff like it's the worst thing in the world. It doesn't bother him in the slightest.

He kisses down my body, hooking his fingers into the waistband of my leggings as he tugs them down along the way.

"You smell divine." He says, licking his lips with his eyes locked on my core. He rips his shirt over his head before latching his lips around my clit. My hips buck off the bed, my greedy pussy begging for more. He wastes no time delivering, as he slips a thick finger into me, then a second, pumping in rhythm with the flick of his tongue. I have the sheets in a death grip as my whole body seizes up and my orgasm crashes through me. I am still trying to catch my breath when I feel the head of his cock nudging my entrances.

"You good Princess?" I nod my head, pulling him in for another kiss. I gasp out a moan as he presses into me. "Fuck Harley, your pussy is heaven." My pussy is heaven? He has no clue how good he feels. Well, how could he? He is huge, I am so full of him, and his piercings, have mercy... they feel fucking amazing. I have never been with someone with piercings before, and boy, was I missing out. He plows in and out of me, over and over, until my insides are vibrating with the need to release. Sliding one of his enormous hands under my ass, he lifts me up to his thighs, changing the angel and stars explode behind my eyes as another orgasm shoots through me. It's not long after I feel him swell inside me as he finds his own release.

He drops his forehead to my shoulder, both of us panting, trying to catch our breath and slow our racing hearts. After we have calmed down some, he places a soft kiss on the tip of my nose, then pulls out of me.

"Stay right there. I'll be right back." I watch as he walks to the bathroom, his tight ass on display. Men should not look this good. It is criminal and unfair. He is back in no time, cleaning me up with a warm washcloth. Holding his hand out to me, he says. "Come on, as much as I would love to just lay here with you for a while, I just heard Xan's truck pull up." I don't even waste time grabbing his outstretched hand. I quickly jump to my feet and pull on my clothes as I run to my bathroom, hoping to make myself look less like someone who has just been thoroughly fucked before my best friend sees me. Jack is laughing the whole time. The fucking asshole.

Maddie is laughing at something Jack has said in the living room while I am still tugging at my hair. I know I have to get out there. I can't hide out in here all night. That would for sure raise some questions. I take a deep breath, then head out to face the music. Maddie smiles from ear to ear when she sees me.

"I was starting to worry that you fell asleep in there. Are you feeling better?" I stare at her for a moment, confusion clearly written all over my face.

"I told her I thought you weren't feeling too well. That you had just up and ran off to the bathroom." Jack says with a shrug. I am going to kill him... slowly.

"Umm yeah, I feel better now. Must have been something I

ate." I say back while thinking of all the ways I can hurt this man. Maybe tie him to the bed when he is asleep, then pull every hair on his ball sack out one at a time.

"Maybe you shouldn't let Jack cook." Maddie throws out, making Xander laugh.

"You're probably right," I tell her, bumping my shoulder into hers.

"Hey, I'm an excellent cook. Right, JoJo?" She is now in Jack's arms, smiling at him.

"The best daddy." She says before kissing his cheek and wiggling out of his arms to go back to playing with the twins. After a few minutes of us just standing around catching up, Maddie grabs my arm.

"Show me what you have done with your new room." She says, pulling me down the hall behind her. No sooner had we walked into my room than she was closing the door behind us and spins around to face me. "Soooo... how has it been living with Jack?" She asks, dragging out the word so for far longer than necessary. I can feel my cheeks instantly heat as though she already knew something happened. I'm sure she does now.

"You little hussy." She squeals, way more excited by whatever she thinks is happening here than she should be. "Is he any good? He looks like he would know how to please a woman." Okay, so maybe she does know what has happened. I should have known I couldn't hide it from her.

"Look, before you get excited, it's just sex, nothing more," I say, holding my hands up in front of me.

"Yeah, yeah. I know both of you. Now answer me. Is he good?" I roll my eyes at her.

"Why is Xander not living up to your fantasies?" I ask her jokingly.

"Hardy Har, Har. You're so funny." She says walking past me and sitting on my bed rubbing her belly. I let out a sigh, sitting beside her.

"I know you are hoping Jack is going to swoop in and give me a family and the world like Xander did for you, and I do not doubt that he will do just that for some lucky woman. It just won't ever be me. You know why Maddie, and besides the fact that I could never give him a family, we can't get along to save our lives, outside of the bedroom, that is." She is just shaking her head at me.

"That is bullshit, and you know it, Harley. The doctors said there is a chance, and if not, he has a daughter whose mother doesn't want her. It's a ready-made family. You are simply scared of letting someone in. I get it really, I do. I was too, but you wouldn't let me give up and I won't let you either," she says, trying to soothe me.

After a moment of silence, I finally decide to give her what she wants.

"He was amazing," I say, bumping my shoulder into hers. "Like really amazing. Did you know he has a Jacobs' ladder piercing?" She looks at me with her eyes as wide as saucers.

"Why the fuck would I know that?" I can't help but laugh at the look on her face. I can't quite tell if it's shock or disgust now, knowing that minor fact about her man's best friend. "You're the worst." She says, then laughs with me. "Now, if Xander catches me looking at Jack's crotch later, it's all your fault," I swear I can't breathe. I am laughing so hard. We finally sober up and she leans her head on my shoulder. "Do me a favor." She is rubbing her belly again.

"What's that?" I ask her. "Don't completely give up on your happily ever after. I'm not saying it is Jack, but someone out there is perfect for you. Don't give up." I force a smile on my face.

"I won't give up, I promise." She doesn't completely believe me; I don't believe myself. A knock at my door interrupts our conversation.

"How does grilled burgers here for dinner sound to you, Angel?" Xander calls through the door. Maddie's eyes light up every time he calls her Angel, and it is the sweetest thing ever. I am so happy for them. They make the best couple, and the twins took to him quickly. You can tell he loves them like they are his own and I love him for it. They spent the first seven years of their lives with no dad, and I know having Xander around is going to be great for all of them. All kids deserve to have two loving parents in their lives.

"Sounds great to me." She singsongs back her reply. I love them, really, I do, but I can already tell tonight is going to be a long-ass night. And all I want to do is crawl into bed, well after I crawl back into Jack's bed for another round. *Maybe. Is this a bad idea?*

The night isn't getting any better. The longer Madds and Xan are here, the more time I have to think about all that can and will go wrong with Jack's and my new arrangement. I realize how stupid we are when I think about it. Someone is bound to get hurt if we keep this up. No good can come from us playing house like this. I need to put a stop to this madness. He's not going to. One of us has to be the adult here, do the right thing, no matter how bad it will suck. And it will suck. I had some of the best orgasms of my life with that man, but that's all it will ever be.

Chapter 11

JACK

I THOUGHT HAVING XANDER, MADDIE, AND THE TWINS over for dinner would help Harley not stress so much about our new agreement. I, however, did not anticipate her telling Maddie about it, and I know she did. I keep catching her staring at me funny and even caught her looking at my junk a time or two, so I am assuming she now also knows about my piercings. It is extremely awkward to have my boy's woman looking at my junk like she's able to see it through my pants. I am honestly surprised Xander has not noticed, or if he has, he hasn't called her out on it yet. Harley somehow seems more uncomfortable as the night goes on, and I cannot wait to get her alone to find out what is troubling her. This situation is too perfect to allow her the chance of talking herself out of it over something silly. I notice her walking down the hall and quickly follow her. I have to find out what is bothering her and find a way to fix it. There is no way in hell I am bringing random women in and out of my house with JoJo here, and I cannot ask Harley to keep her for me to go on the prowl. This is the best option for me. I slip in behind her before she can close the bathroom door. Kicking it shut behind me, I pin her against it, crowding her personal space.

"What has your panties all in a wad tonight, Shadow?" I ask her as I run my nose along her neck. "Was one orgasm not enough to put a smile on your pretty face? If not, I can take care of that right now." I run my hand up the inside of her thigh, torturingly slow. She huffs, pushing at my chest, trying, and failing, to move me away from her.

"This is stupid. We shouldn't be playing with fire like this. I live here and take care of your kid. Jack, at some point, feelings are going to get involved and someone will end up getting hurt." Grabbing her hands, I pin them above her head against the door as I lean in close.

"Let's get something straight, Princess. There will be no feelings, no attachments, nothing more than sex. That's all I have to offer, that's all I want. Don't look at Xan's and Madd's relationship and think that it could happen here. I won't be the prince in your story, Princess. The best I can give you is a dick to ride until you move on with your life, as long as you keep that in mind this," I say, pointing between the two of us with my free hand, "will work perfectly." She glares at me for a moment before she finally responds.

"Fine. Whatever, have it your way, but do not say I didn't try to warn you when lines get blurred." I chuckle at that, which only causes her scowl to deepen.

"That's cute, but again, it won't. Trust me." I let her arms go, picking her up. I move her out of my way so I can go back to our guests. She growls at me as I walk out the door. Or at least I think it was meant to be a growl. It sounded more like a purr.

"You're such an asshole." She huffs before slamming the door. Humm, I thought I was a jackass.

I catch the stink eye from Madds as soon as I walk back into the living room. There is no escaping her wrath, either. She apparently misses nothing.

"Do you have to piss her off every chance you get?" she asks with her arms crossed, and her hip kicked out, showing just how annoyed she is with me at this moment.

"She makes it too easy, Madds, and besides, it's fun. I have to entertain myself somehow." Obviously, that was not the proper response, because Maddie smacks my arm with what I am sure was all her strength.

"Will you just grow up already and stop playing this *'I like this girl. Let me pull her pigtails'* game you have been playing for the past year." Taking a step back and holding my hands up in front of me, hoping to deter any further attacks from the ferocious pregnant woman in front of me. I notice Xan laughing behind his fist and flip him off before I turn my attention back to his angry better half.

"That is not what I am doing, and I didn't start any of this. Remember, she is the one who gave me the cold shoulder at the cookout last July. I just keep swinging back." I say, shrugging my shoulder nonchalantly. She is still not amused. Turning to Xan, she waves a hand in my general direction.

"Fix it." She tells him and he laughs harder.

"There is no fixing him, Angel. You will just have to let them work this out for themselves." He pulls her into his arms, I'm sure, in a feeble attempt to keep her from pouncing on me like a little possessed spider monkey. Pregnant women are scary as fuck. Have you ever pissed one off? They will put the fear of God in you, I swear. She huffs, pointing her finger at me.

"If you knew what she has been through, you would be nicer, is all I am saying. Now I am going to tell my friend bye and offer to let her come stay with us, so we don't have to plan your funeral anytime soon, then we are going home." She pulls out of Xan's arms and stomps down the hallway to find Harley. Xan shakes his head, slapping me on the back as he walks off to JoJo's room where the twins are currently. She wanted them to watch a princess movie with her before bed. Sammie was game for it, Seth, not so much, but when JoJo batted her long lashes at him, he gave in just like I always do.

It's not long before we have all said our goodbyes. They left, and JoJo was finally down for the night. I am sitting in my recliner with the tv on, watching God only knows what, because I can't focus on it. I keep thinking back to what Maddie said. *'If you only knew what she had been through.'* I thought I had kept Ben away from her. I tried my best to, anyway. Hell, I was just a kid myself. I hated that prick from the moment they placed me in that foster home from hell. He always acted like his shit didn't stink' and he was better than me because his parents wanted him. He would fuck shit up and I would get blamed for it. Every. Single. Time. I tried to stay out of his way until Harley showed up, that is. She was so tiny for a ten-year-old. You could tell she had been poorly taken care of, not that you would expect much more, given where we were. She would follow me around everywhere. I never understood why she wanted to be around me so much, but I didn't mind. I started calling her my Little Shadow, which didn't seem to bother her at first, maybe because I said, *'my Little Shadow* and she wanted to feel like she belonged, that I could fully understand. But when I had to start pushing her away to keep her safe, the *'my'* dropped, and Harley started taking offense to the nickname. It killed me to see the hurt in her eyes as I pulled away from her friendship and spent all my time with Ben, not because I wanted to, but because that was the only way to ensure he was never around my Little Shadow. He would have died a slow, painful death if he ever touched her like he planned to do.

The home we were in wasn't that big, and usually Ben had a room to himself since he was their biological kid. However, when Harley was brought in, I got put in the room with him, since she and I couldn't share the same room. I was trying to fall asleep one night about a month into her being there when he informed me. *He hoped she hadn't been touched before because he would love to deflower a pretty little thing like her.* Now, I know what you are probably thinking. *Jack, why didn't you tell his parents?* His parents were not much better than him and thought he could do no wrong. They would never believe me over him, so I did what I had to do to keep her safe. I never told her why I pushed her away and was relieved when they found her grandmother and she was no longer in harm's way. It wasn't long after she was gone; they placed a new girl with us. He didn't show any interest in Tammy, so I thought she was safe. I was wrong. I wanted to puke when I walked in and caught him trying to force himself on her. After yanking him off of her and kicking his ass, he ran off crying to his mom, saying I attacked him for no reason. They believed him over me like I knew they would and called my caseworker to have me moved. I don't think they ever thought that maybe my caseworker would listen to what I had to say, but thankfully she did, and Tammy was placed in another home as well. Charges were placed against Ben, and his parents could no longer foster other children. It is the one time I saw the system work in our favor. Tammy and I stayed in touch throughout the years. She went on to be a social worker herself, hoping to save other kids from a horrible fate. She is an amazing woman and an even better friend. I hope he had never gotten his hands on Harley. I cannot remember a time I wasn't around long enough to where he could have, but then again that was years ago, and there was no way for me to always be with him, especially when I would end up with afternoon detention when he would find a way to place the blame on me for something that he had done.

HARLEY SPENT THE ENTIRE NIGHT LOCKED IN HER room, avoiding me like the plague. I had not heard a peep from her all night. When she finally walked out long enough to go to the bathroom and make herself a cup of coffee, she acted like I wasn't even there. I need answers and I need them soon before I lost my fucking mind. Thoughts of what could have happened to her have been running through my mind all night. I know I hurt her feelings when I pushed her away all those years ago, I do, but no way in hell is she still upset over that. No, something bigger has to be messing with her, but what? And why do I care so much? She is just a piece of ass to me. Well, and my babysitter. It should not bother me so much that she won't even look at me, much less talk to me. But yet, here we are. Maybe it's because I feel guilty for possibly not keeping her safe when she was younger. Not knowing for sure might be the death of me. JoJo wakes up running into the living room.

"Daddy, waffles." She shrieks as a way of greeting me this morning. My lips curl up into a smile as I look down at my precious little girl.

"Are you cooking?" I tease as I pick her up and head into the kitchen.

"No silly, you cook." She giggles. "I go get Harley." She wiggles out of my arms.

"Wait, Little Monster, I think we should leave Harley alone.

I don't think she is all that happy with me today." I tell her, squatting down to her level.

"Why daddy? Did you be mean to her?" She asks with her hand on her hip. I almost laugh, almost.

"No, Little Monster, I wasn't mean to her. We just had a.... disagreement is all." She looks at me, confused.

"Diss-a-what?" she asks, scrunching up her little nose. This time I do laugh. I can't help it. She is just too damn cute.

"You know how sometimes you want to stay up late, and I tell you no, then you get upset with me?" She nods her head yes. "Well, it's something like that," I tell her, not sure of a better way to explain it.

"So, you told her to go to bed?" God, this kid is a hoot.

"No sweetness, I did not tell her to go to bed. The reason for the disagreement is not important. I just think we should leave her alone until she is not upset anymore, yeah?" She taps her finger to her lip, and I crack up again. She picked that up from either Harley, Maddie, or Sammie. They all do that same thing when they are thinking of a way to fix whatever one of us guys have fucked up.

"I know. We take her food in bed. Sammie said her mommy gets big smiles when they take her food in bed." I open my mouth to say no, but then it hits me. She has a good point. Most women like breakfast in bed.

"You know what, Little Monster? I think that is an amazing idea. What do you say we run to the store and grab her some flowers real fast, too?" Her face lights up.

"Me flowers too?" I chuckle, walking her to her room to get dressed. "Yes, you can have flowers too."

It doesn't take long to get to the supermarket in town and JoJo wastes no time in pulling me straight to the flowers. "How did you know where the flowers were?" I ask her as we both start looking for the best ones.

"Sammie's daddy got her mommy some." She tells me, looking at me like I should already know that. I suppose Xan got stuck with the kids on a supermarket run recently. The thought brings a smile to my face. I can only imagine all the things JoJo and Maddie convinced him to buy with just a few fluttery lashes and pouty faces.

"These one's daddy," JoJo says, bouncing up and down with some daisies in her hands.

"Daisies?" I ask. Slowly grabbing them from her.

"Yep." she says, letting the 'p' pop. "Her loves' em,' she told me." She grabs herself some as well.

"Okay, if you say so. Let's go get something to put them in." She grabs my hand walking beside me.

"And candy." She says as she starts skipping through the store. This apologize breakfast is getting expensive and I am not even remotely sure what I am apologizing for. Two vases, two boxes of chocolate, two bouquets of flowers, apple juice, one bottle of wine, and we are finally heading back home. How did breakfast in bed for Harley turned into a treat for JoJo as well? I will never know, but here we are, and she looks mighty pleased with herself for it, too. I am going to have my hands full as she grows up. After pulling up at the house, we head inside to make waffles. It surprised me to see that Harley didn't leave while we were gone. Maybe she fell back to sleep, and we will have time to get everything ready before she wakes back up.

JoJo carries the chocolate, while I carry the tray with everything else on it. I left the wine in the kitchen since I didn't figure she would want it with breakfast, anyway. I knock on the door, then wait for a response. When I hear nothing, I convince JoJo to try. She knocks.

"Harley, I got a prize for you." She yells through the door. Harley's laughter from the other side brings a smile to my face. I am so thankful the two of them are so close. JoJo needs someone like Harley around for all the girly things.

"You can come in, JoJo." She calls from inside and JoJo waste no time swinging the door open, running, and jumping on the bed next to her. This kid knows no boundaries.

"Daddy made you food in bed, and look, look, he got you flowers too." She squeals, bouncing up and down on the bed. "And my got you chocolate. See." She holds the box up in Harley's face to be sure that she sees them.

"Calm down, Little Monster," I say, walking in and handing Harley the tray in my hand. She smiles up at me.

"Thank you and thank you too, Princess." She tells JoJo, kissing her on the cheek.

"Daddy got me flowers too," JoJo says with a huge smile on her face.

"Did he? Will you go get them so I can see how pretty they

are?" JoJo jumps off the bed and runs out of the room as fast as she entered to do just that.

"What's all this for?" Harley asks gesturing at the food and flowers.

"We wanted to do something nice for you." I shrug nonchalantly.

"You wanted me to stop avoiding you is more like it." She huffs out.

"Something like that, Princess." She rolls her eyes at me but doesn't comment further since JoJo has come back in with her hands full. She brought everything she got this morning.

"Daddy got you juice too, but not the same as mine." She announces as she shows Harley what all she got from the store. Harley looks at me, confused.

"It's adult juice. I didn't think you would want it with breakfast." I tell her.

"Oh..." she says before turning her attention back to JoJo. "How about I bring this to the kitchen and we eat together?" JoJo's face lights up.

"Yes, please." She hands me her flowers and chocolate. "Here daddy, you hold this." Then she walks off to the kitchen, leaving Harley laughing and me stunned. Where does she get this attitude from?

Chapter 12

JACK

I NEVER THOUGHT JACK, OF ALL PEOPLE, WOULD BRING me breakfast in bed. Color me surprised when he walked in with not only breakfast but my favorite flowers in hand. I am not sure what spurred his decision to spoil me this morning, other than I refused to speak with him, but that doesn't seem like something that would bother him enough to buy a woman flowers. Especially a woman he could care less about. I have caught him looking at me strangely a few times since we sat down to eat. It's like I am holding a secret he desperately wants the answer to. What? I don't have a clue. I do know I couldn't finish my plate fast enough. I needed to get out from under his watchful eye, and quick. Thankfully, it is Sunday, so Jack will be at home with JoJo all day. This was supposed to be my weekend off anyway, so he shouldn't mind if I dip out for the rest of the day. I head to my room and quickly get ready to leave. I don't know what I will do or where I will go. Anything would have to be better than the awkwardness going on between Jack and me this morning. Jack and JoJo are nowhere in sight when I emerge from my room. Grabbing my purse and keys off the entry table, I head out to my car. I act like I don't see Jack waving to get my attention from over by the tire swing where he is currently pushing JoJo. I simply back my car out of the drive and leave with no destination in mind.

Rose's Scoops is a small ice cream shop on the edge of town. It is one of my favorite places, and as I pull in, I get excited knowing I get to indulge in some amazing homemade ice cream. After letting out a deep breath, I grabbed my phone to see who was blowing it up during the drive over.

> Jackass: Where are you running off to?

> Jackass: I know you saw me trying to get your attention.

> Jackass: So, we are back to you ignoring me again?

> Jackass:...

> Jackass: Fuck it, I don't have time for these childish games.

Me: Calm down, daddy... I didn't see you, and I had some errands to run. It is my weekend off, isn't it? I didn't 'think I needed to run my whereabouts by you.

This man is frustrating. Where does he get off acting like I owe him some explanation about when and where I go somewhere?

> Jackass: What errands? Who are you with? I kinda like you calling me daddy. Can we make that a thing? (Winking face emoji)

> Me: Fuck you.

> Jackass: Tonight.

> Me: Did you need something, or can I go back to what I had planned?

> Jackass: We need to talk.

> Me: About??

> Jackass: Don't worry about it, we'll talk tonight.

> Me: Whatever.

I toss my phone back into my purse and climb out, heading into the ice cream shop. After I have my mint chocolate cone in hand, I sit down, thumbing through my phone. I spend an hour just aimlessly watching TikTok videos, avoiding the fact that I have no life and can't even go home, to my own home, because I now don't have that, either. Why did I let myself get into this mess? I knew it was a bad idea to move in with him from the start. Nothing good could come from a casual hook-up with him, especially with us living under the same roof. Does that mean I won't let it happen again? Probably not. A girl has needs to, you know, and if he is willing to satisfy them, then so be it. I am tired of sitting alone, so I decide to head over to Maddie's and spend some time with her and the twins. Hopefully, they don't mind the company since I ran the battery dead on my phone. I should have remembered to charge it last night. My adulting abilities are lacking at the moment. It doesn't take me long to get to Maddie's. Getting out of my car, I quickly walk up the steps, knock on the door and wait. A few minutes later, Xander opens the door with his phone to his ear.

"She's here." He says into the phone. "Okay man, later." He hangs up and pockets his phone. "Jack was looking for you. JoJo wanted to know if you wanted to go to the park. I reckon your phone is dead." My eyes roll of their own accord. I am fairly sure one of the rules was that he never uses JoJo against me in any way, not that either of us has done a good job of following the rules thus far.

"Yeah, I forgot to charge it. Is Maddie here?" I was confused as to why I hadn't been invited in yet. It is not like Xander to be rude and leave someone standing out in the cold.

"Shit, sorry." He says, scrubbing his hand down his face and stepping aside so I can come in. "It has been one hell of a day. The twins' aunt Hope is here meeting them for the first time." He tells me quietly as I step through the door, causing me to stop dead in my tracks.

"They're who? I didn't know Bret had a sister?" He grunts.

"Neither did Maddie." This is crazy. How does a sister just appear out of nowhere?

"Are you sure, like, is she really their aunt? Why is she here? What does she want?" My voice is starting to rise as I talk, so Xander pulls me back out the door, closing it behind him so they cannot hear our conversation.

"Trust me, I would not let anyone around my family before making sure they were good. Got me?" I nod my understanding.

"I know, sorry. I am just still getting used to someone else watching out for them." He relaxes some at my statement.

"I got Sam's friend to look into her. Hope is really their aunt and now has no other family left. She just wants to get to know them, and you know just belong somewhere. She has been through some stuff that is none of my business to share, or even know, for that matter. And I wouldn't if it weren't for him digging into her past and family." I let out a long breath and shake out my limbs.

"Okay, I'm ready." Xander laughs.

"Whatcha ready for, Rocky? Gonna go in there and clear the house?" I snort, slapping his arm.

"Shut up. No, I was preparing myself to be nice." He is laughing so hard tears are forming in his eyes.

"Damn, I needed that laugh." He says opening the door and ushering me in.

"Glad I could be of service." I don't know what I was expecting as I stepped into the living room but was surprised to see a tiny woman in all black with multicolored hair to be sitting on the floor with the twins playing some kind of fighting game on the PS4. Is it wrong that I feel a little jealous and like she is taking my spot in their lives? And for that reason alone, I don't like her very much. Yeah, I know I am bitter and being petty. They have been with me for the last eight years. I have been their only aunt, the one who helped raise them, and the one who has been around for all the ups and downs.

I plop down on the couch by Maddie. She has a huge smile on her face, watching her kids play and form a bond with their aunt.

"I was wondering when you two would stop gossiping out there and come enjoy the fun with us." She teases, turning her big smile to me.

"We were not gossiping." I huff. I hate that she can always see through my bullshit. Leaning in close, she whispers in my ear.

"No one could ever replace you in their eyes, Harls, you know that, right? They are just gaining another aunt to love. My best friend pulls me into a hug.

"I know, now are you going to introduce me to our new friend?" I ask scooting down to the floor beside Sammie.

"Of course. Harley, this is Hope, Bret's sister, Hope, this is Harley, my best friend." Maddie happily supplies gesturing between the two of us as Xander sits down where I just was, pulling her in close to him. "It's nice to meet you," Hope says, smiling shyly at me with a small wave.

"Nice to meet you, too." I give a little wave as she goes back to the game they are playing. It's not long before we find ourselves in the kitchen making lunch for the twins. Maddie spins on me after placing a PB&J sandwich on the plate in front of her.

"So, you going to tell me why Jack was calling us looking for you this morning?" She inquires with a raised brow and a smirk firmly in place. Rolling my eyes, I shoot back.

"How should I know? He called you. Did he not say?" She waves the butter knife in her hand my way.

"You're evading. What are you trying to hide, Harls?" I put my hands up, playfully surrendering to her.

"You don't have to threaten me with that deadly weapon ma'am I will talk." Maddie and Hope both burst into laughter and Maddie sits down the knife.

"What happened?" She asked, sobering up when she sees my scrunched-up nose.

"Nothing really. I just needed to get out of the house for a while and Sir Jackass didn't take well to me not telling him where I was going." I shrug nonchalantly.

"Xander's friend Jack?" Hope asks, trying to catch up with what we are talking about.

"The one and only." I huff, pouring the twins both a glass of milk.

"He's hot," Hope says, and my head snaps to her. "Sorry, are you two a thing?" She asks, looking unsure of herself.

"Nope." I say, letting the 'p' pop. "You can have him. Knock yourself out." I notice Maddie shoot her a look that says I wouldn't do that.

"Look missy, I told you there is nothing between Jack and myself. Even if I wanted to date him, which I don't, he doesn't want anything other than an easy piece of ass." Hope sucks in a breath and I mentally scold myself. "I swear I wasn't insinuating that you are an easy piece of ass. I would have warned you not to go after him if you seriously showed any interest."

"All good. I didn't think you were." Hope replies with a smile on her face. Maddie rolls her eyes and goes back to getting lunch ready.

"I think you are both full of shit." She says as she puts the plates on the table and calls for the twins to come to eat. We all sit down, and I decide it is time to change the subject. What better way to do just that than to get to know Hope better?

"So, Hope, where are you from?" Maddie gives me a questing look.

"Just a few towns over from here." Hope answers, shifting in her seat.

"Where do you work? Are you looking to move out here?" I ask, tucking into my sandwich, and Maddie kicks me under the table.

"Aww, what?" I ask, rubbing my shine

"Stop interrogating her. You are making her uncomfortable." Maddic huffs, giving Hope an apologetic smile.

"It's okay. I work at a club in downtown Blackstone. I live

close by, and it pays fairly well." She shrugs her shoulders and goes back to eating.

"That sounds like fun," I say as I take another bite of my sandwich.

"It's a job." She replies. It gets quiet for a while, and I worry I may have crossed a line I was not aware of somehow.

"As far as moving here, I would love to, so I could be closer to the twins. I just don't see it happening anytime soon." She finally says, breaking the silence. I smile at her.

"When you decide to, let us know. We would love to have you here and will help you get settled." She smiles brightly back at me.

"Thank you." Then she heads back to the living room with the twins.

"She doesn't like talking about her past," Maddie whispers to me after Hope is out of earshot.

"Why?" She sighs.

"I don't know, but giving who her brother is, I can't imagine it was the best childhood growing up." She has a point there. Not that we know anything about how Bret was raised either, but surely something caused him to be as messed up as he was.

A few hours later, I have made a new friend and said my goodbyes. I never charged my phone, but based on the side glances and smirk I was getting from Xander all afternoon, I would say Jack has been blowing his phone up, and Xander was most likely stirring the pot just to rile Jack up for a laugh. If I have learned anything in this past year, it is that the two of them love to antagonize each other. If I didn't know any better, I would actually believe that they were brothers with the way they act. I pull up outside Jack's and kill the engine to my V. W. Bug. I hadn't even opened my car door all the way before Jack steps out onto the front porch with his arms crossed over his chest. Looking more pissed than I can ever remember seeing him. This is bound to be a train wreck, one that I wish with all I am that I could avoid, but seeing as I fell for his trap and moved in here to help with JoJo, it is one that I will have to face. Taking a deep breath, I step out of my car. He doesn't move a muscle or utter one word as I climb the steps to go in.

"Move Jackass." I huff when he didn't let me by.

"Why is your phone dead?" Somehow, he sounds like he was worried about me. I know he wasn't, though.

"Pardon me?" I ask crossing my arms.

"Why. Is. Your. Phone. Dead? Did you break the charger?" He enunciated each word. Is this man for real right now? Rolling my eyes, I throw my hands up in frustration.

"What is your problem today? No, my charger is not broken. I simply forgot to plug it up last night and didn't grab my charger when I left. I also don't remember agreeing to answer to you." His nostrils flare and he has his jaw clenched so tight it is twitching. I frankly don't give a rat's ass how pissed off he is. I don't have time for this. Nor do I want to deal with a man child pitching a fit because his booty call didn't give him a play-by-play of her day. Without another word, I spin on my heel, heading back to my car. I will come back when I am sure he is in bed. With any hope, things will be back to normal by morning. He calls my name, demanding I not leave as I open my car door. I flip him the bird and hightail it out of there. Dealing with his bullshit is the last thing I want to do today. My new plan, find a place to get wasted.

Chapter 13

JACK

IT IS ALMOST TWO IN THE MORNING. TWO IN THE fucking morning, and I have not heard a word from Harley since she left. I called Xan; she did not show up over there either. She finally charged her phone. Not that she will answer me, but she told Madd that she was okay. They, however, will not tell me where she is.

'She's fine Jack, let her cool off. She will come home when she is ready to.' Bull fucking shit. Xan wouldn't be calm sitting at home waiting if it were Maddie, now, would he? Nope. *'That's different.'* He reasoned. "Maddie is my universe; Harley is just your babysitter, remember?" Asshole, I have never wanted to bust his lip quite like I did right then. He knew it too, judging by the laugh following the snarl from my end of the phone call.

'You finally ready to admit she means more to you than you like to claim?' He seriously had the audacity to ask me that. As a

matter of fact, no, no, I do not. Why you ask? Because it fucking scares me shitless, that's why. I shouldn't care where she is, what or who she is doing. Yet here I am, pacing my living room at TWO in the morning, worried about some women that should be none of my concern. You learn quickly not to let feelings get involved when you are dispensable to everyone around you. My heart going rogue and attempting to get attached has never been a problem before now. So, tell me what has changed. Is JoJo making me soft? I would not say I'm in love with Harley, but in like with her, could that be a thing? Maybe. Fuck, JoJo is making me soft.

The sound of someone pulling into the drive catches my attention and I storm outside to meet Harley at her car. Only her car is not in my driveway. I don't know the man helping My Shadow out of his truck, and rage quickly consumes me as I stalk in their direction. I don't give her feet time to hit the ground before I am snatching her out of his arms.

"Who the fuck are you?" I ask, placing Harley on her feet beside me. She wiggles out of my arms, giggling and tripping over her own damn feet as she answers.

"This is D, my best FWB." The fuck is she talking about?

"What is an FWB?" Not sure I want to know, but I asked anyway. D shakes his head at Harley.

"Go to bed, Harley, you're drunk." He says flatly as he walks around to the driver's side of his truck.

"Friends with benefits." She tells me. "I'm not that drunk, D," she yells at his back.

"You are and stop trying to start shit, Harley. Go to fucking bed." I step away from Harley to stand in front of this D. Who names their kid D, anyway?

"What the fuck happened tonight?" It is taking everything I have not to acknowledge the fact that he has fucked my girl. He holds his hands up between us.

"Look, man, I didn't have anything to do with that." He states, gesturing in Harley's direction. "She was already piss poor drunk when I ran into her at the Club. I had to get a friend to keep an eye on her long enough to get my truck, then I brought her straight here. I didn't know she was seeing someone, or I would have told her to call you for a ride and just made sure she was safe until you got there." Glancing over my shoulder at Harley, I murmur my response.

"Thanks for making sure she made it home safe man, we will go grab her car later." I hold my fist up for him and he taps his to mine before climbing into his truck.

"No problem, man. Keep an eye on that one. She is wild." He laughs. *Don't I know it?*

"Wait, it's Sunday. What club is open on Sundays?"

"Pussy Cats,' in Blackstone." He shuts his door and pulls off into the night. Sighing, I turn back to Harley to see her glaring at me like I have done something wrong.

"Come on Shadow, it's time to get you in bed." She huffs her disapproval but heads to the front door with me, anyway.

"What is your problem today, Jackass?" I wrap my arm around her, to steady her going up the stairs.

"My problem? I am not the one who showed up drunk at two in the morning, Shadow." She scrunches up her nose.

"I really fucking hate that name." She pushes out of my arms and almost falls flat on her face as she steps through the door. I just barely catch her before she hits the ground.

"Do you, do you really?" I ask her teasingly.

"You know I do. How hard is it to get my name right?" She huffs, crossing her arms, and pouting at me.

"It's a nickname, Princess. I have no problem getting your name right." I point out.

"Nicknames are for friends." She throws back, rolling her eyes and stumbling again.

"We were friends when I gave you that nickname, were we not?" I ask with my brow raised.

"Yes, but then I wasn't good enough to be your friend anymore. You threw me away, just like my mom did." The sadness in her eyes damn near kills me. God damn, I didn't know my pushing her away hurt her that badly. It's time I tell her the truth.

"I did not throw you away. Fuck... Do you not think it killed me to see the pain in your eyes every time you looked at me? My little Shadow, it gutted me every day to push you away." I whisper, smoothing her hair out of her face.

"Then why? Why did you push me away?" She asks me, confusion written all over her beautiful face.

"To protect you." She looks up at me, even more, confused by my admission.

"From what? You?" Shaking my head, no. I drop my forehead down to hers.

"No Shadow, not from me. You'd never needed protecting from me. I could never hurt you. I was protecting you from Ben. I had to keep you safe and push you away from me, so you were never around him. That was the only way I knew how to do that. I was just a kid myself, baby, I didn't know what else to do" Confusion still mars her beautiful face as she blinks up at me.

"Why would I need saving from him?" Having this conversation at this hour of the morning with a drunk Harley nonetheless is the last thing I want to be doing.

"Come on baby, let's talk about this tomorrow, when you are sober, and it's not so late." When I turn to walk her to her room, she digs her heels in.

"No, I don't want to go to bed. Tell me what you are talking about, Jack. I am not even that drunk anymore." She huffs, crossing her arms and tapping her foot, waiting on me to give in to her demands. Sighing my defeat, I pull her behind me to the couch. Pulling her to sit beside me, I start telling her the story.

"When you came to stay at the foster home, they placed me in Ben's room. We had never gotten along, much less shared a room. I am still not sure if he said it just to see what I would say or do, or if he planned to. Given what happened after you left, I think he would have gone through with it. Anyway, not long after you got there, he told me and I quote, *'I hope she has never been touched before. I would love to deflower a pretty little thing like that.'* I couldn't let that happen to you, so I did the only thing I could think to keep you safe."

We sit in silence for a while; I wait while she processes what I just told her and the reality of who he really was sinks in. I thought maybe she didn't believe me, that she thought it was just a lie to cover up for being an asshole all those years ago. That is until she climbs into my lap cradling my face in her palms and I see the tears in her eyes that break my heart just like they did all those years ago.

"Thank you, Jack, for making sure I was safe. Even when it wasn't your place to." Using my thumb, I swipe away the tears that broke free.

"It was my place to protect you. You're My Little Shadow. I had to protect what's mine." She wraps herself around me completely as she crashes her lips to mine. Her kiss is a bit sloppy and forceful. When she grinds her hips down on mine, I break the kiss, leaning my head on her shoulder.

"As much as I want you, Princess, not tonight. You have drunk too much, and I know that what I just told you is a lot to take in. I don't want you to regret this. It's time for bed, beautiful." She looks offended momentarily before climbing out of my lap and heading to my room. Does this woman just not listen to a word I say? After a few moments, I follow behind her, only to find her curled up in my bed, half-asleep. Shaking my head, I strip down to my boxers and climb in beside her, pulling her into my arms. In no time at all, we are both asleep.

I WAKE UP A FEW HOURS LATER TO HARLEY'S HOT mouth wrapped around my cock, sucking me deep down her throat. Holy hell, that feels good.

"Fuck... Princess," I grunt, thrusting my hips up, causing her to gag. Wrapping my hands in her hair, I guide her mouth up and down my shaft until I can't take anymore. Pulling her head back, she releases me with an audible pop. Her smirk is mischievous when she meets my heated gaze. Pulling her up my body, I quickly flip her onto her back so that my body has hers completely caged under me.

"You're being a naughty Little Shadow this morning," I growl, nuzzling into the crook of her neck.

"Your Little Shadow," her whispered words formed a smile on my face as I nip at her ear.

"Always My Little Shadow," I tell her as I begin my slow descent, kissing down the length of her glorious body. She moans out my name like a prayer the moment my tongue connects with her already soaking wet cunt. I devour her like a man starved for his next meal as her legs clamp down around my head. The groan pushing past my lips tips her over the edge as she cums on my tongue. I lap it all up, savoring the musky flavor of her release. Crawling back up her body, I leave a trail of kisses along the way until I am settled between her legs, the crown of my cock nudging her, begging for permission to sink balls deep into her.

"Please, Jack." She whimpers, lifting her hips. Slowly, I sink into her one inch at a time, peppering kisses on her face.

"You're so beautiful, Harley," I whisper against her cheek. Pulling out to the tip, I pause, looking down into her eyes. Never losing eye contact I move in and out of her at a much slower pace than I have before, enjoying every little catch in her breathing, every whimper that passes her full lips, every scrap of her nails on my back, every flutter of her inner muscles around my shaft. This is different, more intense than I have ever felt before. I'm not sure what shifted or what is happening between us. What I do know is that I don't think I could ever let this woman go. And that scares the shit out of me. Her eyes roll back in her head as she comes apart under me and I follow her over the edge. We lay there completely entangled in each other, catching our breath, and slowing our pounding hearts. I finally untangle myself from her, rolling over to lie beside her. I pull her to my chest and softly kiss her head.

"Let's get some more sleep, baby," I whisper into her hair. I have almost dozed back to sleep when I feel her wiggle out of my embrace, climb out of bed, and sneak out of my room. As soon as she leaves me, I feel her absence, and I know at that moment how truly fucked I am. I wasn't supposed to let my feelings get involved here. How did I let this happen?

Chapter 14

HARLEY

SOMETHING FELT DIFFERENT WITH JACK THIS MORNING. I cannot quite place my finger on what it was, but it was there. In the way, he looked at me, the way he touched me, the gentle way he took me like I was precious to him. I had to fight the tears that wanted to break free from the tenderness in his eyes as he stared down at me. I had to get out of there. The moment his body relaxed completely beside me and was fairly sure he was asleep, I slipped out of his arms and snuck off to my room. I tried to get some more sleep, but my mind was running overtime at what it could have all meant. When I came to terms with the fact that there was no way I was going to get any more sleep, I hopped into the shower and got an early start for work. I am ready for work with enough time to grab myself a coffee and breakfast on the way in. With any hope, the caffeine will help to keep me awake, since I got little sleep last night. Something tells me that if I leave without speaking to Jack, he will blow up my phone all day again. I tiptoe past JoJo's room, so I don't wake her, and sneak into Jack's room to let him know I am heading out. I stumble to a stop when I notice he is not only ready for the day but is sitting stock still on the edge of his bed with his head in his hands. Slowly, I make my way closer to him, placing my hand on his shoulder. I watch as his facelifts to mine, and he does his best to hide the fear lingering in his eyes. Was this morning too much for him to work through as well?

"What's wrong?" I ask. He tries to force a smile on his face as he grabs the front of my scrubs and pulls me in between his open legs.

"All good, Shadow, just a little tired is all." His smile takes on a more realistic look.

"Sorry about that." He yanks me down to the bed rolling on top of me.

"I'm not sorry." He tells me as he lowers his lips to mine, kissing me with more passion than I thought he was capable of. When his hand slips under my shirt to cup my breast, I break the kiss, giggling.

"Stop Jack, JoJo will be awake any minute and I have to get to work." Grunting his agreement, he pushes off the bed. Holding his hand out to me, he helps me up.

"You're right, come on." He says, leading me to the door. When I have my bag and keys in hand, he gives me a quick kiss, telling me to have a good day and see me out the door.

I could not concentrate all day. I am so confused by how

Jack has been acting today. He even text me to ask if I wanted him and JoJo to bring me lunch, claiming to have been out and about already. When I told him I had already had lunch, which was a lie, he told me he couldn't wait for me to get home, that they missed me, and he had big news to tell me. Why did things have to change? Why couldn't he just keep things sex only? Instead, he had to go and talk about the past and what he did for me. As he called me his Little Shadow, I saw feelings that I can't even explain, nor do I want to try and figure out in those eyes of his. It was like he was gazing into my soul. This is not what we discussed, no feelings, only fucking. He was supposed to fuck me fast and hard, say all the dirty things that guys that don't give a rat's ass say. Not slow and gentle, telling me how beautiful I am. And then he has the AUDACITY to offer to bring me lunch to work. LUNCH. AT WORK. Like he is my loving boyfriend or some shit and then he goes and says he misses me. Seriously, what the fuck? Has he forgotten how a fuck buddy works? Heaven help me because I liked every damn bit of it. God knows I had the biggest crush on him back when we were kids before he pushed me away. He was my first crush and my first heartbreak. I spent years hating his guts for just throwing me away like I meant nothing, just like my mom did all the time before her addictions took her away from me completely. Her heroin addiction was always the most important thing to her. I couldn't even say I came second. No, that would have been the men who supplied her with her vice. The ones she ran to for every fix she needed. She would rather be high when she was feeling down and lonely. It was easier than facing her own life. I was just the mistake waiting at home for her, needing things she didn't want to provide, like food, clothes, shelter, hell, even an iota of love. However, none of that is important at the moment. What is important is figuring out how to get things back on the right track with Jack, because even if I wanted a serious relationship with him, or anyone else, I have nothing to offer.

I don't know what I was expecting when I got home today, but a car I didn't recognize in the drive was not it. To make matters worse, when I walked in... there was a bombshell blonde sitting on the couch with her head tossed back in laughter, sitting way too close to Jack. What is this I'm feeling? Jealously? Maybe? Ugh... It tastes bitter on my tongue. I cannot be jealous; we are hardly even friends. What is there to be jealous over? I clear my throat as I drop my bag on the side table to get their attention.

"Oh, good Harley, you're home," Jack says with a huge smile on his face as he stands up from his seat. I want nothing more than to knock that grin completely off his face right now.

"Who's this?" I ask with way more malice than necessary, given the fact that he is a grown man and can do as he pleases, plus we are nothing to each other. So why does this sting so bad?

"Wow, Shadow, what's wrong?" Jack whispers as he tries and fails to pull me into his arms.

"Answer." I bark out, crossing my arms over my chest and

taking a step back. The mystery woman stands to her feet tentatively.

"I'm terribly sorry. I didn't mean to cause a problem." She starts to say more before Jack interrupts her.

"You didn't Tammy. I don't know what has gotten into Harley today. She is not typically this catty." Oh. No. He. Did. Not. Did Sir Jackass just call me catty? Lord, please help me to not be caught when I dump his body later tonight.

"Did…" I don't get the chance to finish my sentence because he undoubtedly has a death wish and chooses this moment to talk over me.

"This is Tammy, a friend who also happens to be the social worker helping me to get full custody of JoJo. She came by to inspect the place and make sure JoJo's needs are being met as well as to let me know they have gotten ahold of Brandy, and she is coming to sign the paperwork." Oh… I fucked up. How do you backpedal after this cluster fuck?

"Umm. Hi Tammy, it is nice to meet you." As sweetly as possible, I say it as sweetly as I possibly can. "I was just surprised. I am so sorry. Um… that was rude of me." She smiles, holding her hand out to shake mine.

"You're good. I would have acted the same way." She laughs lightly before picking up the bag at her feet. "It was nice meeting you, and good to see you again, Jack. I will call when Brandy is in town and ready to sign over JoJo. You both have a wonderful evening."

Jack walks Tammy out to her car. No doubt to apologize for

my poor behavior. I am currently hiding out in my room, hoping to avoid Jack for the rest of the evening, when I hear him stomping through the house. With any luck, he will just say goodnight to JoJo and head to work. Maybe even forget this happened by the time he gets home. My door slams into the wall as he storms toward me. I don't even have the time to register that he is in my room, much less sit up before he is standing between my legs, leaning over my sprawled-out form, caging me between him and the bed.

"What the fuck was that all about, Shadow?" He growls, and not the sexy *'I want to devour you'* growl he usually uses with me. No, this is an *'I am pissed off'* growl. Again, I know, I fucked up, big time. Not only did I make myself, the caregiver when Jack works, look hotheaded, and maybe a tad bipolar but I also showed, that even though I will deny it until my dying day, I also have feelings for him, and I got jealous. I do not get jealous, ever, like never.

"I don't know," I whisper, turning my head away from his stare. Praying he can't read the lie on my face.

"No, don't give me that shit, you know. You just don't want to admit it." Grabbing my chin, he turns my face back to his. "You are cute as fuck when you're jealous." He says, nuzzling my neck, eliciting a moan from me.

"I wasn't jealous, I was just worried about JoJo." I lie, yet again. Like I said, I will NEVER admit to him I was indeed jealous. I would rather have a full-body wax, I mean from the top of my head to the soles of my feet, full-body wax.

"Keep lying to yourself, beautiful. I have to get to work, but I expect your sexy ass to be in my bed waiting for me when I get home. Got me." He places a quick but heated kiss on my lips before leaving me laying here a panting, wanton mess. Oh boy, I am in big trouble. If the huge smile on my face and the blush I can feel crawling up my neck wasn't a dead giveaway, the butterflies taking flight in my stomach are. This is bad, so terrible. Will I do anything to stop the inevitable train wreck? No, no, I will not. He is just too damn hot, and so damn good in bed. I might as well enjoy the perks while I have the chance to and suffer the consequences when they arise because I have no doubt the fallout will be ugly and painful as well as unavoidable. I only hope that my heart can survive it and that JoJo doesn't get hurt in the crosshairs.

JoJo and I have had the house to ourselves all day. Longer than a usual day, since Jack had a sizeable tattoo that he is working on today. He left early to get his station set up before the customer arrived for their six-hour session. We have had a lazy day. I love Saturdays. I don't have anything I have to get done. Just chill at home in my pajamas with this amazing little girl. We have had breakfast, went out to water the flowers we planted last week, and now we are settling in to watch some new movie she has been wanting to see. Armed with a bowl of popcorn and M&M mix in hand, we press play. Not even halfway through the movie, there's a knock at the door. I leave JoJo watching the movie and go answer the door.

"How may I help you?" I ask politely as I open the front door and take in the woman standing in front of me. Currently looking at me in disgust. Must be one of Jack's many women. Rolling my eyes, I cross my arms over my chest, leaning against the door frame. "Well..." I ask, still waiting to find out what the hell she could want.

"Jack here?" She asks me, looking me up and down like she is sizing me up or some shit. How the hell does she think she is?

"He's at work. Can I help you with something?" The hussy just stares at me for a moment, like she is having trouble processing what I have just told her. Is she high?

"Look, I'm Brandy, Jo's mom. I'm here to pick her up. Jack didn't want her anyway, and I found a buyer... I mean... someone who wants her." Did. This. Bitch. Just say she has a buyer? Like JoJo is fucking property. The fuck.

"Are you crazy, or just stupid?" I question her as I reach behind me, grabbing my keys from the hook and locking JoJo inside. No way in hell is she getting to my girl. *My little girl? Fuck yeah, she is. I might not understand what my relationship is with Jack right now, but that little girl is mine!* This bitch would have to kill me first to get her hands on my girl.

"I don't know who you are, or why you seem to think you have some kind of say in the matter. But that's my daughter, and I will be leaving here with her." Brandy tells me, trying to stand her ground. I laugh in her face, a bitter laugh.

"I'm going with stupid. You're stupid. That's the only thing that makes sense here. You do realize that the courts would even disagree with that statement, right? You abandon that little girl with a man she had never met, whether or not he was her dad. You didn't know and now you also just stood here telling me you found a buyer for her." I let my eyes go wide, hoping she understands just how fucking crazy she is.

"I didn't mean it like that... I... I meant that I found a man who... umm... wants to adopt her. He's not far from here, has been good to me, taking care of me since I have been in town. I know he will take care of her, too." She tells me, scratching at the track marks on her arm. Now I get it. She's a drug addict.

"Not happening. What you can do though is leave here. Call Jack, or go by Xan's Ink and see him, even come back with the cops. Frankly, I could give a fuck less what you do, but you will not be setting eyes on that little girl, much less leaving here with her." I inform her.

"Listen, bitch," she seethes, pointing her finger in my face, causing a smirk to tug on my lips. "I will be leaving here today with that fucking kid; do you hear me? I need a fix and she is my meal ticket to get it. You will not stand in my way." She slaps me across the face. Mistake. Big mistake, I'm not one to throw the first punch, but I sure will throw the last one. Before she even sees it coming, I catch her with a right hook to the jaw. She stumbles back a few steps before righting herself and coming back at me. I sidestep her, grabbing the back of her stringy hair. Feeling very homicidal, I slam her face into the door, breaking her nose. She falls to the ground, covering her face, crying out in pain. I give her a few swift kicks to the side because she has pissed me off to that level, then call the cops and Jack to let them know what is going on.

It doesn't take long before Jack is peeling into the drive, the cop cars right behind him with their sirens blaring. He checks on JoJo and me before explaining to the officers that he has surveillance cameras that run at all times to protect his girls and that they could pull them as evidence. They informed me not to leave, because they may have more questions. Cop talk, for *'we might decide to arrest you after all.'* That's fine, let them. As long as my girl is safe, that's all that matters to me. It's nice to know, after the fact, that Jack has security cameras set up around the place. He swears they are just on the outside to protect us from other people. I rolled my eyes and reminded him, that I'm a big girl and can protect myself, but he wouldn't hear it. Apparently, he feels it's his place to protect both of us. Alpha men, they drive me insane. The officers made their way back over to me and Jack and informed us that Brandy was being arrested. She had been screaming about the man she had promised JoJo, too. Bitch was so high she just kept saying *"I need her, she's my meal ticket."* I just think her brains are so fucking fried from whatever she's been injecting in her arms that she is absolutely batch shit crazy. The police were finally able to cuff her but were unable to get her to tell them where he could be found. Such a shitty person, if you ask me.

Jack walks over to me after he speaks to the arresting officers. He explains how JoJo came into his life and has all the documentation to back it up. She's still screaming for JoJo from inside the police car. The officer looks at her and finally yells "Shut the fuck up!" earning a laugh from me. The police assure Jack that they will take care of Brandy and inform Tammy of what transpired. Jack asks the officers to send Tammy a copy of the arrest paperwork along with a copy of the footage from his cameras. The police agree to get it over to her as soon as possible.

"I...uh...I don't even know how to thank you," he says with tears in his eyes and his voice cracking.

"Look, Jack, I know we have had our differences, but there was no way in hell I was going to let that bitch or anyone else come in and take JoJo away," I explain to him. I wanted to yell at him that she was *MINE* and no way in hell some high skanky ass bitch was going to take her away from me. Jack might take her someday and that is a risk I am willing to take to be a part of JoJo's life, but that is a problem for another day.

"I'm just glad Brandy was alone, and I was able to stop her. Just know that when JoJo is with me, I will protect her like she is mine." I stared him in the eyes so he could see my anger and protectiveness.

"I know, thank you though for protecting her," he says as he engulfs me in a gripping hug.

Chapter 15

JACK

FOR SIX MONTHS NOW JOJO HAS LIVED WITH ME, HAS been a part of my life, and has become my world. Last month Brandy signed over all of her parental rights, JoJo was officially mine. Not that she had much of a choice after she got arrested and Tammy presented to the court the video of her admitting she was going to sell JoJo. No one can take her away from me now, and I have to give a copious amount of credit to my friends for that, all of them. They helped me to get my shit together, to be sure JoJo had everything she needed, from the material things to someone at home with her while I work. They stood by my side in court when Harley and I both testified against Brandy. Yes, life is definitely looking up. I never pictured myself wanting to be a dad, but now I couldn't picture my life without her. It's crazy how much your outlook on things can change in such a short amount of time. I still wish I could offer her an actual family, but I can't change the fact that it's just me. It is what it is. She seems happy and I know she gets plenty of love and attention. She wants for nothing, other than maybe wanting a mom. I'm doing the best I can. Fortunately, Harley is around to help where a mom would be needed, although I can't guarantee she will be here when JoJo reaches her teen years and will undoubtedly need her the most. I know that Maddie would help JoJo and me if we needed her to, if and when Harley ever decides to leave us. However, it's just not the same. Let's not focus on the things I can't change at the moment. We have a baby shower to get to and finally find out the sex of baby Carter.

"You ready to go, Little Monster?" JoJo has been looking forward to the baby shower all week and can barely contain her excitement.

"Yes!" she squeals, jumping up and down.

"All right then, let's head out." The gifts are in my truck. I have JoJo's bag with extra clothes, just in case, along with our swimsuits and towels. I think I have everything.

"Where's Harley, daddy?" JoJo asks, looking around as we lock up the front door.

"She is already there. She left early to help Maddie get everything ready." I tell her as I scoop her up into my arms and place her in her booster seat. Quickly, I buckle her in and head around to the driver's seat. Backing out, I carefully maneuver around all the equipment and materials Justin and his crew left here. They started building my house a few months back. It is coming along nicely, and I can't wait to see what it looks like when it's finished. JoJo and I are both excited to move in. I let JoJo pick out the paint for her walls. She picked a light blue and ask if they could paint some white fluffy clouds as well. Justin joked her walls were going to end up looking like the Simpsons intro. I have to agree, but if that is what she wants. Who am I to say no? Whatever makes her happy. That's the most important thing.

It doesn't take us long to get to Xander and Maddie's place. We seem to be the last ones to arrive. The driveway is full of cars, and I can hear the joyous laughter coming from the backyard as we get out of the truck and head inside. After walking in, JoJo and I head straight to the backyard, where everyone is celebrating. I stop dead in my tracks when my eyes land on Harley. Her eyes are wide in amazement, with the biggest smile I have ever seen spitting her face open. Her hand is on Maddie's ever-growing belly. My guess is baby Carter is kicking up a storm for them. I try rubbing away the ache in my chest at the sight that forms in my mind. Harley having her own baby shower with my hand rubbing her swollen belly as our baby kicks. What the fuck? Shaking my head, I try to dislodge the image that has materialized and made itself at home there. It's only when I realize that the thought of Harley pregnant with my child brought me happiness instead of scaring the shit out of me. It hit me. I'm in love, I am fucking in love with Harley Gains. Have mercy. I was not expecting to be slapped in the face with that realization today. Taking a steadying breath, I step further into the party, hoping my newfound discovery isn't written all over my face.

"Hey man, I was wondering if you two were going to show up," Xander says as he slaps my back.

"Yeah, this Little Monster couldn't decide on the perfect princess dress," I tell him as I tussle JoJo's 'air. Xander throws his head back, laughing before crouching down in front of JoJo, so they are at eye level.

"Tell me, sweetheart, was it your fault or Dad's that you were late?" He asks, catching her when she throws herself into his waiting arms.

"Daddy's," she supplies happily before running off toward Seth and Sammie, who are playing on a tire swing.

"Traitor," I call out. She isn't paying attention to me at all. Turning back to Xander I ask, "What happened to finding out the gender of baby Carter? Everything is yellow."

"Angel wanted to cut a cake for the reveal. Harley went and picked it up this morning. She thought it would be more fun that way." He tells me as we walk over to a table filled with finger foods.

"I bet the twins are excited to find out." He laughs again, shaking his head.

"They placed bets. Sammie says a girl, Seth says a boy, I say, boy. Maddie said she doesn't care, as long as they are healthy." He tells me with a proud smile on his face. We fill our plates with cocktail sausages and cubed cheese as we look out at all of our friends and family gathered around. I've never been to a baby shower before today. It amazes me at all the decorations used for something so simple. Everywhere I turn, there are pale yellows, blues, and pinks. People laughing and chatting away, congratulating Madds and Xan again on their bundle of joy, that we are all gathered to celebrate.

Not long after the kids have eaten; Maddie has opened all the baby gifts and we are now ready to cut the cake. Everyone is excited to find out the gender of baby Carter. JoJo is bouncing with excitement in my arms. I am not entirely sure if her excitement is due to the cake or learning the gender of her new playmate. A hush goes around our family and friends as Maddie and Xander cut the first piece of cack together, revealing a pink interior.

"It's a girl," rings out around us as everyone cheers. JoJo squeals loudly and I feel as though my eardrums may rupture. After sitting her down, she runs straight to Sammie. The both of them are spinning in circles, giddy that another girl is being added into the folds. I burst out laughing when they stick their tongues out at Seth. He tries to keep a look of displeasure on his face but fails miserably when they both wrap him in a hug, telling him he will be the best big brother a girl could ask for.

"So, another girl," I say to the happy couple as I wrap Maddie in a hug.

"That means we get to try for one more, right Angel?" Xan says, wagging his brows at Maddie. She softly smacks him on the chest while giggling.

"I don't know about all of that. Maybe if you carry and have the baby, we could talk about it."

"Sounds like a no if I have ever heard one." I joke as Xan pulls Madds into his arms. Whispering something in her ear that causes a blush to rise up her neck. I excuse myself from the lovebirds in search of JoJo. When I finally spot her, my chest aches at the sight. She is sitting on Harley's lap on the ground as they both happily eat some cake. Harley gently wipes some crumbs from the corner of JoJo's mouth before placing a kiss on the top of her head and snuggling her closer. I wish we could have what Xan and Madds have. To create our own little family and forge an unbreakable bond like Xan and Maddie have. Even with all the crazy shit, life has thrown their way. I doubt that Harley would ever be willing to try for more. Hell, I didn't realize 'til today that I could want more with her. She may be willing to share her amazing body with me, but that will be all she would ever be willing to share. I want more, I want all of her. Mind, body, heart, and soul. I need her so tangled in me, in my life, in my love, that even if she wanted to, she could never dislodge herself from my world. She wouldn't know where her world ends and mine begins. We could have an epic love. One that could rival any other on this earth. If only she would be willing to give a piece of shit like me a chance. Harley looks over her shoulder at me, her soulful eyes lock with mine, and she smiles sweetly at me. My heart constricts in my chest, and I rub at the pain absentmindedly while smiling back at her. This woman will be the death of me, of that, I am sure.

ALL OR NOTHING

JoJo was exhausted by the time we made it home from the baby shower. I wasn't sure she would last even long enough to get a bath and brush her teeth before she passed out. Now that I tucked her snuggle into bed, I am getting into the shower. Harley stayed to help Madds and Xan put away the baby's new things. The hot spray of the shower helps to loosen my tight muscles, but does nothing to lessen the ache in my chest. The pain of never being able to truly claim Harley lives there. I think back to all the hell I gave Xan last year when he fell in love with Madds and laugh. I had no clue how fast love could sneak up on you. There was no way for me to. Love isn't something I witnessed in its purest form during my childhood. It was always just a fairytale, something that would always be out of my reach. Until My Little Shadow came back into my life. Now it's the only thing I crave. My head falls against the shower wall as I feel Harley slip into the shower behind me. I have to fight back the admission of my love for her as her arms snake around my waist and she leaves a trail of kisses down my spine. When her small hand wraps firmly around my now rock-hard length, a guttural moan escapes my throat.

"Is this for me?" She purrs from behind me. Removing her hand from my cock, I spin around to face her. Pinning her to the wall, I nuzzle into the crook of her neck. I breathe in her sweet scent. I now know is a mixture of sweet pea body wash and the perfect deliciousness' that is purely her.

"Only for you, Shadow, only for you," I whisper before sucking the shell of her ear into my mouth and biting down hard enough to cause her to gasp out my name. Placing my hands under her ass, I lift her so she can wrap her legs around my waist. Lining me up perfectly to enter her tight, warm, little cunt. To claim her in more ways than she is ready to be claimed, in more ways than she is willing to let me claim her. Claiming her is my intention. She doesn't know it yet, but she will forever be mine. I will make her my wife, fill her with my seed, and together we will create a family. One that neither of us had the pleasure of enjoying as children. If I, have it my way, she will adopt JoJo, and be the only mother she will ever need in her life. Slowly, as to not hurt her, I push into her inch by inch. Her head drops back so hard against the wall that it makes a loud thud, that almost drowns out her moans of pleasure. For the first time in my life, I make love to a woman.

"Oh, fuck Jack, you feel so good." She whimpers as I thrust in and out of her at a steady pace. Leaving gentle open-mouth kisses along her neck, across her jaw, and up to her lips. Claiming her mouth with a passionate kiss. I don't know how much longer I can hide my true feelings for this woman. I need to get a grip on myself before I scare her away. She needs time to wrap her mind around this. I need to make her see how great we could be together on her own. Trying to tell her wouldn't work with her, she is too headstrong for that. No, she has to come to that conclusion for herself. Then and only then would she be willing to give in to what I know we could be.

"Cum for me Princess, let go, cover my cock in your juices," I growl into her neck, no longer able to hold off my impending orgasm. She moans out my name as her walls spasm around me, milking my release for me. I slam into her, to the hilt, coating her womb with my seed, and for the first time, hating that she is on birth control.

"Damn, Princess," I mutter before peppering her face with kisses.

"Yeah, I needed the release too." She says before untangling her leg from around my waist. Pulling out of her, I place her on her feet and make sure she is steady before I step back from her. "Thanks for that hotshot." She says with a smile on her face before she climbs out of the shower, leaving me standing there watching her leave just as quickly as she came. God damn, I need her to realize that I am it for her. I am tired of her going back to her room when she is finished with me. I want her in my bed, in my arms. No, I don't want it. Like my next breath, I need it. I don't know when I became such a pussy, wanting to declare my feelings and shit, but damn if Harley doesn't make me want a future with her. Like my next breath, I need her. I wish she would realize I would be everything she needs me to be for her if given the chance.

Sighing, I turn off the shower now that it is freezing cold and climb out. Drying off, I quickly pull on my briefs and head to bed. Thoughts of how to convince Harley to give me a real chance filter through my mind as I fall asleep.

Chapter 16

HARLEY

I can't sleep. No matter how hard I try, I just keep tossing and turning in my bed. What was that? I wasn't ready for bed, but after that moment with Jack in the shower, I had to get out of there. This is frustrating. I wasn't done with him. I hadn't had my fill yet. Now I am laying here still horny, not able to sleep. Why? The hell if I know. I could have just been reading into his gentle caresses. He may have just been tired or... hell, I don't know, was maybe trying something new. Fuck this, I am going back in there. To hell with overthinking and not getting what I need out of the man. Throwing my covers back, I climb out of bed and sneak my way into Jack's room. He is already asleep. The covers are barely covering his waist, his sexy, bare chest on full display. Judging by the tent under the covers, I'd say he was having a pleasant dream. Slowly, as to not wake him up too soon, I remove the covers from his waist. Settling myself between his spread leg, I position myself so my face is right above his massive cock that is currently trying to push its way out of the opening of his tight black briefs. Snaking my hand into the opening, I wrap my hand around his solid length and tug his massive member free. Quickly realizing my mistake when he sucks in a hissing breath at my icy touch. I go completely still, holding my breath, waiting to see if I have woken him up too early. When I am sure he is still fast asleep, I let the breath out that I was holding and drag my tongue across the bottom length of his shaft. My tongue grazes over those amazing piercings that drive me wild, up to his slit that is now dripping with pre-cum. His salty flavor burst on my tongue.

"God damn, Harley. That mouth of yours." Jack groans out, wrapping his fist in my hair as I suck him deep into my throat. His moans and mumbled curses spur me on as I move up and down his length, swallowing him down. Before I know what is happening, he has my mouth ripped off of him. Then I am pinned beneath him on the bed, with him grinding into my core while nipping and kissing along my neck. His rough, callused hands have my arms pinned above my head in a tight, bruising grip. This, this is what I needed. Him to have his way with me, to use my body in a way that only he has been able to. I need him to be rough and demanding as he takes my body to heights, I never knew I could reach before he came along.

"Please, Jack, fuck me hard," I beg as he teases my opening with his bulbous head. Only pushing in the tip, then taking it away just as quickly.

"Oh, now the Princess wants to have some fun. What happened earlier when you hightailed it out of the shower as soon as you got off?"

"I just needed a moment to... hell, I just needed a moment for myself." I can feel his smile against my neck like he knows something that I don't know.

"If you say so, Princess." He mumbles as he presses into me, filling me so full it almost hurts, but damn, does it feel so fucking good. He plows in and out of me, showing no mercy. The tenderness he had shown earlier in the shower is nowhere in sight. He is fucking me now, and it's only now that I realize why it felt so different earlier. He was making love to me. It is something I have never had, that's why I didn't recognize it for what it was. Was it intentional, or was he just tired? I'm pulled from my thought when he roughly grabs my jaw and crashes his mouth down on mine. I am painting for air when he finally breaks the kiss.

"Is this what you needed, Princess? You just needed to be dominated, used?" He asks as he slams into me once more.

"God yes." I moan.

"Cum for me Princess. Give it all to me." He growls out as he lifts my leg higher, changing the angle so he is so deep I am teetering the line between pleasure and pain. Stars explode behind my eyes as my orgasm crashes into me.

"Fuck, Jack." I cry out. He kisses me again, swallowing my cries of pleasure. He stills, pushed in to the hilt. I can feel him swell inside of me before he paints my slick walls with his release. He collapses beside me, pulling my back to his front and holding me close.

"Sleep, Princess. I will make sure you are up and back to your room before JoJo wakes up." I wouldn't usually stay in his room, but after the busy day we had, and now two explosive orgasms, all I want to do is sleep. Jack whispers into my hair as I am dozing in and out of sleep.

"I love you, My Little Shadow, more than you could ever know, more than I ever thought was possible. One day, I will make you my wife and the mother of my children. This I promise you." Tears fill my eyes as I try my best to hold back a sob, and he places a soft kiss on my head before he falls asleep.

I LAY AWAKE ALL NIGHT. NOT ABLE TO FULLY WRAP MY head around Jack's sweet whispers when he thought I was asleep. I can't stay here. If I stay, I will have to explain to him why we could never work and that's not a conversation I want to have with Jack. It was hard enough to tell Maddie. Wiggling out of his embrace, I stand by the bed and look down at the one man I know could capture my heart if I let him. Taking in his peaceful, yet strong features, I memorize him the best I can, before sneaking out of his room and into mine to pack my most important things and get the hell out of dodge. He can find someone else to keep JoJo. I will miss that little girl like crazy, but I have to protect my heart at this moment. It is going to kill me to abandon that little princess but, for once, I have to put myself first. It doesn't take me long to get all of my things together. Thankfully, I only brought a few things other than clothes. After I have everything I can fit, loaded into my V.W. Bug, I write Jack a quick note before leaving.

Jack,

    I hate to do this on such short notice, but I have to move out. This is all becoming too much, and I just need to remove myself before things get too far out of hand. I will miss JoJo dearly and hope that in time I can still be a part of her life, even if it is a small part. I will also miss you, believe it or not. I will see if I can get Xander and Sam to come and get the rest of my belongings. I couldn't fit it all into my tiny car.

    I am terribly sorry to leave like this; I know it will not be easy to find someone else to be here for JoJo. I can keep her at Madds and Xan's place for the time being until you can find a replacement if you need me to.

    P.S. Thank you for giving me the chance to get to know such an amazing little girl. You are a wonderful dad and will do just fine without me.

Also, thank you for protecting me all those years ago and being such a great friend, even when I didn't know that was what you were doing.

Always,
Your little Shadow

BY THE TIME I PULL INTO MADDIE AND XANDER'S DRIVE, my eyes are red and puffy from all the crying I have done. I didn't realize how hard it would be to walk away. Not only from JoJo but also Jack. He holds a piece of my heart, even if I can't admit it to him. How could he not? He is such an amazing person. Dragging myself out of the driver's seat, I make my way to the front door and knock. Hoping that I am not waking them up this early in the morning. It is just now half-past six. The sun hasn't even been up long. I didn't know where else to go. Maddie is all that I have had for a long time now, and now, not having a home to go back to, I didn't have anywhere else to turn.

"Harley, what's wrong?" Maddie asks as she wraps me in her arms. My eyes fill with tears all over again. Now I am bawling my eyes out on my best friend's shoulder. "Shh. It's ok, come on. Let's go inside and we can figure out what is going on and how to fix it." She soothes me as she rubs my back.

"Thank you Madds." Sniffling, I try to clean away the tear streaks from my cheeks. It does no good, as I can't stop the tears from flowing. Maddie takes my hand, pulling me through the house and into the kitchen. After she has me sitting at the table with a box of tissues in front of me, she makes us both a big cup of coffee, then sits beside me, wrapping her arm around my shoulder.

"Now, tell me, what has my best friend showing up on my doorstep this early in the morning crying her eyes out?" Maddie questions.

"I am so sorry for coming by so early. I didn't know where else to go. I didn't wake you, did I?"

"No, silly, and don't worry about it. What happened?" She asked again. I knew she would not give up.

"Jack said he loved me," I whisper.

"Let me get this right. Jack, Xander's hot as fuck friend Jack, told you he loved you and it made you cry?" she says, looking at me like I have lost my mind.

"I am going to pretend I didn't just hear you say my friend was hot. If you two can give me just a moment to fix me a cup of coffee, I will be out of your way, and you can get back to your talk." Xander grumbles as he walks into the kitchen.

"Oh, shut it you, you know you are the only man for me. I was just making an observation." "Maddie says giggling.

"I know Angel," Xander says after his cup of coffee is poured. Turning around, he places a kiss on the top of Maddie's head. "Do I need to kick his ass, Harls?"

"No, no ass-kicking is needed. At least not for him. He did nothing wrong." I tell him.

"Alright, if you two need me, just holler. I will be on the

back patio." He kisses Maddie again, then heads out the back door.

"Spill," Maddie demands as soon as the back door has closed behind Xan.

"He didn't tell me he loved me. He more or less whispered it to me when he thought I was asleep. The *'I love you'* wasn't what started the tears, though. It was him promising to marry me and give me kids. That did me in." I drop my head down on the table with a sigh.

"Oh, Sweety, I am so sorry. I know how hard the talk of kids is for you. Are you going to tell him?" She asks.

"Not a chance in hell," I answer with a bitter laugh. "Do not give me that look. I know what you are thinking. Telling Jack does not change the possibility of me being able to have kids."

"No, but it explains to him what is going on and you could still be a family, the three of you. What could improve your chances of having his baby is going to the doctor." She says, giving me a pointed look. I know she is right. I have been thinking more and more about going back to the doctor, doing all the tests, and coming off of my birth control. See if maybe I could finally have babies of my own.

"Do you love him, Harls?" Maddie asks, breaking my train of thought.

"Yeah, I think I do," I whisper, still not completely ready to admit it out loud.

"So, tell him." She tells me, giving my hand a reassuring squeeze.

"I can't, not right now. Look, can I just stay here with you guys for a while? I don't mind sleeping on the couch, just until I can find another place to rent." I ask, hopeful she won't keep pushing me.

"Stay as long as you need." She tells me, giving me a tight hug before getting up and cooking breakfast for the twins.

IT HAS NOT BEEN EASY AVOIDING JACK THE PAST FEW weeks, and today will be a true test of my patience. It is the annual Fourth of July cookout at the Carter house. Jack will be here, of course, and it's not like I can just leave. For the first two weeks of me being here, Jack would bring JoJo to me every day to babysit, but I guess me hiding every time he would come over proved too much for him, and now Maddie's mom babysits more often than not. I hate losing more time with JoJo, but I understand why he is pulling away more. Since I left his house, I have not tried to talk to him, not even once. I don't answer his calls or reply to his text. He had the nerve to tell me to stop acting like Maddie. That made me laugh a bit. It doesn't seem like that long ago we were trying to get Maddie to talk to Xander, trying to get them back together. Oh, how the tables have turned. Now it is Maddie and Xander are playing the go-between. Telling me what Jack is saying, how he is feeling, trying to convince me to talk to him, to give this a chance. They don't get it, no one does. It's not that I don't want to give him a chance. It's not that I don't think we could be great together. I know we could. The problem is that I still don't know if I can give him everything he wants. I have stopped taking my birth control. Now I am just waiting for the test to see if my eggs are still good. My OBGYN said as far as the scarring went, it looks like they got all of it the last time, so all good on that front. But what happens if they say everything is fine and I still fail to carry full term? Not only would losing another baby devastate me, but so would Jack when he realizes I am not good enough for him. It would rip my heart out if he decided that I wasn't enough and left me. I know there is no way for me to know for sure how he would respond without first trying, but I am too scared. That is the only outcome my evil little brain keeps playing on repeat. Torturing me, making me feel less than enough.

I slip my feet into the new silver sandals I bought to go with my American flag printed sundress. It is short and flowy and barely reaches mid-thigh. Choosing to have my swimsuit under it so I will not have to come back inside to change when I am ready for a swim. I throw my long hair up in a messy bun. I didn't feel like messing with it today. And my face is free of makeup, much like it has been for the past few weeks. I just cannot seem to find it in myself to worry about what I look like these days. Depression, that is what this is, depression at its finest. Honestly, I thought I had moved past this, coped with the knowledge I would never have a family of my own, at least as much as someone could. However, I know that is not the only thing that weighs heavily on my heart. No, that fantastic man and his adorable girl's heartbreaking with my absence is also a huge cause of my current anguish.

'Get it together, Harley. They will be here at any moment. You do not need everyone to see you crack under pressure. It will only make things worse.' Straightening my back, I take a deep breath in through my nose and release it out of my mouth. *'Let's get this show on the road. You are strong, you are beautiful, you have got this.'* I give myself one last pep talk before heading downstairs to join my friends and family in celebration.

Chapter 17

JACK

My breath catches in my throat as I step out onto Xan's back patio with JoJo in hand. Harley looks so fucking beautiful, with her head thrown back in laughter. Her little American flag dress flowing in the breeze. JoJo wastes no time dropping her hold on me to run straight for her. She has missed her like crazy, much Like I have. I know I look like a fool, standing here with my eyes glued on Haley as she bends down to scoop an excited JoJo into her arms. Anyone can see the love and happiness shining in both their eyes. Harley is twirling her around and peppering kisses all over our little girl's face. I mean my, my little girl's face.

'She didn't want you, Jack. Get it through your thick-ass skull already. As a matter of fact, she has done everything in her power to avoid the likes of you.' God, it hurts. I gave Xan hell for this. Now I understand what he was going through. It is like I have been gutted. Except, I cannot sit around numbing my pain in a fifth of whisky like he did. I have a little girl counting on me. I have to keep pushing forward, planting a fake ass smile on my face, and acting as though I don't have a care in the world. When in reality, I feel as though I am slowly dying on the inside. It makes it worse when JoJo asks when she is coming home, or when she says she misses her new mommy, and that her new mommy was better than her old mommy. I thought my heart would bleed right out on my kitchen floor when she asked me if it was something she had done. If she had been a bad girl and ran Harley off. I had to reassure her it was nothing that she had done and that even though I call her My Little Monster or Gremlin, she is the best kid a dad could ask for. She still wanted to know why she left and unfortunately, I don't have an answer for her, hell I don't know the answer myself. Maddie tells me to talk to Harley, who will not speak to me, and Xander says he doesn't know, which I tend to 'believe. I am sure he knows as much as ' do. She wasn't asleep like I thought she was when I opened my big ass mouth and told her my secret. One that I should have kept hidden just a little longer. My delectation of love scared her away, but why? That is the million-dollar question, isn't it?

"Hey man, how's it hanging?" Justin asks walking up to me and slapping me on the back. I turn around, smirking at him, seeing that Xan and Sam are standing next to him.

"A little to the left, about halfway down my leg." The guys laugh at my remark.

"We will never really grow up, will we?" Xan asks in between bouts of laughter.

"Not if I can help it," Justin says, tipping his beer back and draining the contents.

"Speak for yourselves. I am all man." Sam grunts.

"Who's been lying to you, man?" Xan asks Sam, laughing even harder. I needed this time with the guys.

"Fuck you, asshole." Sam counters, shoving Xan. Justin is right. None of us will ever really grow up. Which is perfectly fine by me.

"So, has she spoken to you yet?" Xander asks me as we all grab a beer and gather around the grill to get the food started.

"Nah, JoJo ran right to her when we got here. I have been hanging back. She will talk to me when she's ready." I tell him with a shrug of my shoulder.

"Another one bites the dust," Sam mutters from behind his beer. "Guess I am the last man standing."

"Justin isn't seeing anyone. Are you?" Xan asks as he flips the burgers. Justin just stares off in the distance, not answering.

"Maybe not, but he is still caught up in that ex of his." Sam states before almost dropping his beer. "Who is that?" He questions pointing at Hope, who just walked into the party.

"Who? Oh, that's just Hope. She is the twins' aunt. After that dickhead found himself in the hospital, she went to see him, didn't know anything about them before that. She said she made him tell her what he knew and then looked us up. Just wanted to be a part of their lives. She is a sweet girl. A little wired but sweet." Xan offers.

"The aunt that Big D looked into for you?" Sam asks, still not taking his eyes off of Hope.

"Yep, the one and only. Why? Big D said she would not be a problem, sure she had a bad go at it when she was younger, but wouldn't cause a problem. Do you know something he doesn't know?" Xan questions, the spatula in his hand now in a death grip. I can see the anxiety rolling off of him in waves. Thankfully, Sam notices as well and clears the air.

"No, man, nothing like that. She just looks familiar is all, I can't place' where I have seen her though." Based on the way he tracks her every movement, I'd say he remembers very well where he ran across her, and if the fire in his eyes is any indicator, it's not a pleasant memory. Why can't the women in our lives just be simple?

"Who's Big D?" I ask, the name sounding vaguely familiar.

"A friend of mine, he is a part of the Phantom Reapers MC. I think Harley had a thing with him for a while." Sam supplies and it clicks where I had heard the name before. He was the guy that dropped Harley off that night she left pissed at me and had gotten drunk. The night I told her the truth about why I pushed her away all those years ago, the night that she started becoming so much more to me than just a fun time and live-in nanny, I just didn't see it yet. I was blind to what she truly meant to me. I'm not anymore. She is who should be in my life. The one woman worth making my wife.

The only woman I have ever loved and the one I want to be the mother of my children. Now I just have to make her see it, too.

By the time food is done and everyone has eaten, I have noticed that not only has Sam disappeared again, but Justin and Becky are nowhere to be found. I scan the group again. Still nothing. It's normal for Sam to up and disappear, but not so much for Justin and Becky. At least they haven't been at each other's throats like usual. Maybe Justin will have better luck with his girl than I am having with mine. When I spot Harley heading inside, I quickly get to my feet and follow her. I am so fucking tired of her acting like I am not even here. Looking over me and walking right past me like I am nothing. This shit ends today. She will talk to me whether she likes it or not. I watch her round the corner as she heads up the stairs. I hang back for a moment, listening to where she is heading. When I hear her stop walking, I swiftly make my way up. She is leaning against the wall between Sammie's room and the nursery. Her head leaning back against the wall, her eyes are closed, and she is rubbing her chest over her heart. Much like I have found myself doing a lot lately. Quietly, I make my way over to her. Wrapping my arm around her waist, I haul her over my shoulder and stomp the few feet into the nursery. She screeches, slapping at my back.

"Put me down, damnit." I kick the door closed, let her tight little body slide down the front of mine, and pin her to the door.

"You know, you have a bad habit of caging me against

doors?" She points out with a mixture of sadness and rage in her eyes.

"You have a bad habit of ignoring me instead of talking through whatever is bothering you. It doesn't leave me much choice now, does it?" I counter, moving in closer to her so that my body is pressed firmly against hers. God, all I want to do is lean in and take her plump lips with mine.

"Trust me. You do not want to know what's bothering me." She seethes, jabbing her finger into my chest.

"That is where you are wrong, My Little Shadow. I do want to know what is bothering you. I want to know why my falling in love with you caused you to run for the hills. Hell, is the thought of being with me that fucking unbearable? I know I am disposable, but fuck, am I terrible enough to make you run like the devil's hounds are chasing you?" She deflates before my eyes. All the anger she was holding onto is now gone, and in its place is a look of despair.

"It is not you, Jack. Do not ever say something like that about yourself again. You are amazing. It's me."

"Don't give me the *'It's not you, It's me,'* bullshit speech, Harley. Just tell me what I did to fuck up. What can I do to fix it? You are killing me, Princess. I know I said I wouldn't be the prince in your story, and I'm not trying to claim I could ever be good enough to be, but fuck, I will try every God damn day if you let me."

"Stop, Please Jack, just stop." She cries, burying her face in my chest. "You did nothing wrong, Jack. It is seriously me. I just... I can't talk about it. Not right now."

"I did nothing wrong, but yet you still found it so easy to walk away from not only me but Jo..." She cuts my words off, slapping me across the face.

"Don't you fucking dare use that precious little girl against me, Jack." Her anger is making another appearance as she bangs her fist against my chest, cursing me for all I'm worth. "You have no fucking idea what you are talking about, asshole. No fucking right to use her against me. I love that little girl like my own, Jackass." Crashing my lips to hers successfully cuts off her rant. I can't take it anymore. I have to taste her on my lips. Need to feel her pressed against me. To know that in some way, she feels at least a fraction for me of what I feel bone-deep for her. She doesn't have a clue what she does to me, what she truly means to me. When she tangles her fingers into my hair, I pull her in closer, deepening the kiss. This is what I have been missing. The feeling of having her in my arms once again, the feeling of pure love. She has to feel it too. Once I am certain she can feel just how much I love her, do I break the kiss, leaning my forehead against hers.

"I love you, Shadow. Please tell me what to do to fix us. I am sorry, whatever I did wrong, I am so fucking sorry."

"You are not listening, Jack. You can't fix it; you didn't do anything wrong. I just need some time to figure something out, okay? Just give me some time, please." She pleads with me, tears filling her beautiful green eyes. I can feel my tears burning at the back of my eyes as I take a step away from her, giving her the space and time, she is asking for.

"Okay, baby. I'll walk away. You can have all the time you need." She moves away from the door, and I walk out, not once looking back. I can't make her tell me what is going on anymore, then I can make her love me in return.

I head back outside to round up JoJo. The love of my life has been prancing around all damn day, talking to everyone but me. I can no longer stay here watching, not knowing how or if I can fix whatever is going on between us. Will she ever open up and tell me what caused her to run away from me, from JoJo? I am left wondering if she could possibly ever love me, or if I will always be nothing more than a notch on her bedpost, a mistake she wishes she could erase. Getting blackout drunk right about now sounds pretty fucking tempting. Just enough to numb the pain and be able to breathe without my heart aching, but I can't because I have a little girl depending on me to keep it together. Maddie must see the defeat on my face because she makes a beeline for me as soon as I step out the back door.

"Hey, is everything okay?" She asks sweetly, pulling me to the side.

"Fine, just going to get JoJo and head out. It has been a long day." I answer, trying to force a smile on my face. Judging by the grimace on Maddie's face, a smile is not what I managed. Oh well.

"JoJo actually wanted to stay the night. How about I send Xan over later to get her overnight bag and you take a break?

Sammie would love to have another girl around, and I think you need it." She tells me with a sympathetic smile on her face.

"I can't just dump my child off on you because I am having a shit day, Madds," I tell her as I step around her, heading for JoJo.

"You are not dumping her off on me. I am asking to keep her for the night. Every parent needs a break now and then. It doesn't mean you are not doing everything right; it just means that you are human." Her lecture has now gained Xan's attention, and he is blocking my path.

"Go home man, I will be by later. Maybe see if Sam and Justin want to meet up as well. We can have a guy's night, shoot the shit like old times. Let JoJo stay here." I sigh, letting my chin drop down to my chest. I can feel my friends staring at me, wondering if I will give in or fight them on this.

"Fine, but if she gives you any problems, call me." Maddie rolls her eyes at me.

"She won't be a problem at all. Now get going." She shoos me away. I almost crack a smile. Almost.

"Can I at least tell her bye?" I ask with my brow raised.

"Sure can, if you think you can wipe that miserable look off of your face long enough, so you don't worry her." Maddie shoots me a stern look.

I quickly tell JoJo bye and I love her, then head out. When I climb into my truck, I can feel eyes on me. I look up to Xan and Maddie's balcony and see Harley's tear-filled eyes shining right back at me. If it is killing her too, then why the fuck is she putting us through this? Putting my truck into reverse, I back out of the drive and spin tires hauling ass out of there. I try to shake all thoughts of Harley out of my mind as I make my way across town, heading straight for the liquor store to buy my weight in alcohol. With any hope, I won't feel this immense stabbing in my chest by sundown.

A FIFTH OF JAMESON, A CASE OF BUD, AND TWO GREASY pizzas in hand, I walk in my front door and collapse on my couch. How is it that I can still smell Harley's perfume everywhere in this God-forsaken house? It is bittersweet. On one hand, I love the smell and the woman it reminds me of. On the other hand, it fuckin' kills me to have a constant reminder of what I can't have. I knew better than to allow myself to get attached, to fall in love. It wasn't meant for me, I'm disposable and I knew that going in. There is no one else to blame but myself. It was only a matter of time before Harley came to her senses and realized she was too good for me. Opening the Jameson, I take a long pull straight from the bottle.

"It's a good thing I thought to grab pizza on the way here. No way in hell two will feed all of us." I hear Xander say as he walks in with four pizzas in hand. Sam and Justin were right behind him with more beer.

"How are you three planning to get home if we are drinking

all of this?" I ask, gesturing at all the booze now sitting on my coffee table.

"The plan is to drink 'til we pass out. No need to drive home. Maddie has the kids for the night. Said she might even call the other girls and see if they want to make it a ladies' night at our house." Xander says, plopping down in my recliner, a slice of pizza and beer in hand.

"I'm not sharing my bed with any of you." I point out digging into the pizza myself. The guys all laugh before tucking in to eat. We spend the next hour talking about sports, my new house, and the name choices Madds and Xan have for baby Carter. It was only a matter of time before they ask about Harley and me. I knew it was coming but also hoped it wouldn't

"You really love her." Justin points out, always helpful.

"Good job, Captain Obvious. You figure that out yourself, did ya?" Sam asks, laughing. It's hard not to laugh with him. He always has a smart-ass remark for everything. Justin flips him the bird before popping open another beer for himself.

"Yeah, I really love her, and she could not care less about me." I sigh, opening myself another beer as well.

"Not true," Xan tells me, taking a swig from his beer. He just shakes his head as I raise my brow, waiting for him to elaborate. "I'm not telling you, she will when she is ready to. I'm not supposed to know, just happened to overhear her and Maddie talking one day. Just don't give up. Give her time. She will open up to you once she has it all straight in her head." Xander says with a pitying look on his face. That does nothing to help me feel better.

"Enough girl talk. We are here to get plastered. This is only making to buzz wear off." Sam huffs and Justin grunts his agreement. We spend the rest of the night drinking and playing poker until we pass out. Harley was still on my mind the whole damn night. I have it bad, and I fear she is the one woman I can never get over. If she chooses to not give us a chance, I will spend the rest of my life pining over someone I can't have. Fuck my life.

Chapter 18

HARLEY

"Harley, wake up. Aghh…" I bolt upright on the couch, as Maddie's cries of pain fill the room around us.

"Breathe Angel, breathe." Xan coaxes Madds as he rubs his hand up and down her back. "Her contractions are five minutes apart. We are going to head to labor and delivery. Do you think you can get the twins up and meet us there?" He asks me as he bends down to grab their go bags.

"Yeah, sure, not a problem." I scramble up from the couch, almost toppling over when my blankets get tangled around my feet. Xan and Madds chuckle at my struggles to right myself.

"You don't have to rush Harls, it could still be hours before Rosie graces us with her presence." She informs me as she cresses her swollen belly. Just then, a look of pain crosses her face as another contraction hits and tries to regain control, breathing through it.

"Good job Angel, keep breathing. Just like that. You are amazing, you know that." Xan is so amazing with her. You can tell how much he loves her in every little thing he does. If I didn't love them both so much, I might just be jealous of them. Who am I kidding? I am completely jealous of their love. I am so caught up in my thoughts, I didn't notice that they had made it to the door until Xan speaks again.

"Right, we are off. It's only five-thirty. If you want to let the twins sleep for another hour, that's fine. No need for them to sit in a waiting room for hours. I will call Tracy, Dan, and Pops on the way. I am sure our parents will want to be there the whole time."

"Gotcha, I will make sure they are up, fed, and out the door by seven. Do you need me to bring anything with me.?" I ask Xander as I follow them out to his truck. I guess it's a good thing he put the car seat in there the other day.

"Nah, I think we have everything. If we end up needing something, I will text you." He tells me as he lifts Maddie up and places her in the passenger seat of his jacked-up Chevy.

"All set Angel, you ready to go bring this beautiful baby girl into the world?" Maddie's eyes sparkle with love for Xander.

"So ready." She tells him, rubbing her belly. He places a quick kiss on her lips, closes her door, then heads around the truck and climbs into the driver's seat. I watch as they disappear down the road before heading back inside and getting ready myself. While getting my things together, I send off a group text to all of our friends.

ALL OR NOTHING

> Me group: You guys, we are having a baby today. Get to the hospital ASAP.

> Becky group: OMG, this is so exciting.

> Justin group: Letting the crew know, then I am on my way.

> Sam group: Just pulled up to a drop off. When I am finished, I will head that way.

> Hope group: I will try to make it. I might be late.

> Jackass group: OTW, I will swing by the shop and put up the notice that we will be closed for the next few days.

> Jackass: I'm surprised you added me to the group text Shadow. You have been doing everything in your power not to talk to me.

> Me: Let's not do this today, Jackass. We have more important things going on.

> Jackass: We can be there for our friends and still work out what's going on between us. Don't use Rosie as an excuse to ignore everything.

I throw my phone in frustration. I can't believe he started already, and today of all days. Today's not about us, it's about Maddie, Xander, the twins, and their new bundle of joy they are bringing into the world. I do not have time for his shit today.

'Try and do something nice, Harley. Look at what it gets you.' That man frustrates me to high heavens, I swear. I think he finds some sick, twisted pleasure in it or something. I quickly get myself dressed and ready to go before heading up to the twins' room to wake them up.

"Sammie, Seth, wake up. Rosie is coming. We need to get going." They both hop out of bed, more than ready to meet their little sister. I head back downstairs to cook up a quick breakfast for us. After we have consumed our breakfast and cleaned up, we head out the door. It doesn't take long to get to the hospital and almost everyone is there when we walk in. A quick look around tells me Sam and Hope are the only ones who have not made it yet. I know what is holding Sam up, but I'm not sure about Hope.

> Me: Hey, Hope. I was just checking in to see if everything was okay.

> Hope: Yeah, all good. I had a flat tire, just got it fixed. On my way.

> Me: Okay, drive safe.

Dropping my phone into my purse, I move further into the waiting room. Watching all of our friends and family talking and cutting up while we wait for Rosie to grace us with her presence. It is nice to see everyone together and getting along. It has been months since we have had to step in to diffuse an argument between Justin and Becky. They don't hang out, that I know of, but at least they aren't at each other's throat.' Jack, JoJo, Sammie, and Seth are sitting over to the side, watching something on Jack's phone that has them all cracking up. Justin and Becky are sitting closer to the doors that lead to the back where Xan and Madds are, not really talking to one another, but being civil. I even caught Becky throwing him a smile a few times. Me, I am sitting here all alone. No doubt Jack is mad at me for brushing him off again. I just cannot deal with him today. There is enough on my plate right now, between work, doctor's appointments, and tests. I just need some time. Why can't he understand that? Well, it's not like I have explained it to him.

"Hey, we have a baby yet?" Sam asks as he takes a seat beside me. I don't miss the glare that Jack shoots his way when he drops his arm around the back of my chair.

"Not yet, still waiting," I tell him as I lean my head on his shoulder. It's not long before Xan walks out, letting us know that Rosie is here, and she and mommy are doing great. Hope has finally shown up and now we can go see the new addition to our ever-growing family. We all follow Xander down the hall to Maddie's room. "Oh, she's beautiful," I whisper as I step up to the side of the bed. Maddie offers her out to me. Cuddling her to my chest, I coo at her. God, I want a baby.

"She's perfect," Maddie whispers, pinching at her chubby little leg. I don't get to hold Rosie long before everyone is demanding their turn. Reluctantly, I hand her over to Hope, who is bouncing on her heels with excitement over her new niece. I catch Jack staring at me again, a look of longing in his gaze. This is going to be a long-ass day.

I HAD ANOTHER OBGYN APPOINTMENT TODAY. THE final verdict, everything looks great. My eggs are healthy and fertile, there's no scar tissue left behind from my other miscarriages. They were able to get it all with that last surgery. As far as they can tell, I should be able to carry full term, with no issues. Should be, there's the keyword. They still cannot guarantee it, and that scares me shitless. I want nothing more than to be a mom. Rosie, being here, has only cemented that fact. The question is, am I strong enough to take the chance of risking yet another miscarriage? Or would I feel fulfilled enough by adopting? If I gave this thing with Jack a try, would adopting be enough for him? Or should I just give up? Do I tell Jack to just move on, that there is no way we could work and forget about ever being a mom myself, or do I give us a chance to try? How do I choose? How do I know what path to take that won't annihilate me in the end? I don't think I am strong enough to face another loss like that and keep going. But I also don't think I'm strong enough to push Jack away much longer. See, the thing is, I do love him. I can pretend all I want that it was just lust. That lines got blurred because we were so close. Living in the same home may have had a hand in us falling in love with each other, but it doesn't change the fact that the love is there and can no longer be ignored. Today is not the day to make this decision, though. Today, we are dress shopping for Maddie and Xander's wedding. Poor Maddie is still struggling with the thought of the dresses not fitting right this soon after giving birth, but neither of them wants to push the date back. Maddie keeps saying that she would be fine with just going down to the courthouse. She says she doesn't need anything fancy. Xander, however, will not hear it. He is adamant that she gets a real wedding. Rather, it would be a small get together with just close family and friends, but she will have one.

Currently, I am sitting in the waiting area of the bridal shop with Hope and Becky. Maddie is in the dressing room trying on all the beautiful gowns we selected. It took us damn near two hours to get here. Hope's drive wasn't nearly as long, seeing as she lives closer than we do. We have already chosen our bridesmaid dresses, well I am the maid of honor, but we still all wanted our dresses to match. Dusty rose, V-neck, off the shoulder, A-line dress with a front slit that damn near reaches my hip. It is a beautiful dress, even if I think the V-neck is cut too short and shows more cleavage than should be excitable for a wedding. It was Maddie's favorite and since it is her wedding; she gets what she wants. We all three-look fabulous in them, if I do say so myself. When Maddie steps out from behind the curtain, my jaw drops. She looks like a princess. Her dress is a beautiful ivory, V-neck princess ball gown, with a court train, and tulle lace. She does a spin for us with a huge smile on her face.

"It has pockets!" Maddie exclaims in delight, causing us to all bust into a fit of laughter.

"You look like a princess." She frowns at me. "Stop that. Why are you frowning? You look beautiful." I tell her, confused at why she would be frowning.

"I was going for an angel, not a princess." She huffs, plopping down on the seat beside me.

"Princess, Angel, what does it matter? You look absolutely gorgeous, and Xan's jaw will drop when he sees you. Seriously, he will catch every fly within a one-mile radius." I tease, making her laugh. No doubt she is thinking back to their first date when I made a similar joke about him catching flies if he didn't close his mouth.

"That man is smitten with you, Madds. You could show up in a potato sack and he would still tell you how beautiful you are." Becky supplies.

"You look amazing, girl. I hope I look half as amazing as you do if I ever get married." Hope adds. Maddie's smile is huge at this point.

"Thank you, guys. You have no clue how much it means to me to have all three of you here with me today. It was nerve-racking bringing Sammie up here by myself to look. She found her dress, but I couldn't decide on anything. I almost called Xander and canceled the whole thing."

"I still don't see why you came alone." I point out.

"You all had to work, and I didn't want to not have a dress." She says, crossing her arms over her chest.

"Well, we are all here now. You have found the perfect dress and look absolutely stunning. So, what do you say we go grab a bite to eat before we head home?" Becky suggests. We all nod our agreement. Maddie goes back behind the curtain to change while I pay. She is not going to like me buying her dress, but I offered to help her parents since they have helped pay for the venue we rented for the night, along with everything else.

As I suspected, Maddie was not too thrilled that I paid for her dress. After I explained it was my wedding gift to her, she calmed down a bit. Becky offered to buy dinner and Hope was paying for our mani-pedis, which also helped as well. We spent the better half of the day just hanging out and laughing our asses off. I am so glad Hope is now a part of our circle. She fits in perfectly. I wish she would let us come visit her sometimes, but she always turns us down, saying her place is too small for us all to get together and instead comes to us. I keep feeling like she is hiding something from us, and I only hope it won't bring any trouble our way. Xander said he had her checked out, but what if they missed something? My family could be in danger. I try to shake those thoughts from my mind as they creep in. Last year was a lot for all of us, and we have come a long way. It is hard not to worry after something so bad has already happened, but it isn't the time 'to think negatively. We have a wedding coming up; we have so many things to be grateful for and to celebrate. Life is good—well, mostly. I still have some things to work out.

Chapter 19

JACK

THE DAY HAS COME. NO, NOT THE WEDDING, THE bachelor party, and I am under strict instructions not to have any strippers. Which is oddly fine by me since the only woman I want stripping for me refuses to even speak with me, still.

'*Give me time.*' Harley said. '*She will come around, you'll see.*' Xander said. '*She loves you too, Jack. She just needs to figure out some things on her own.*' Maddie said.

Here I am, the fool who believed she would come around. Nothing, three God damn months and she still will not talk to me. Unless you count the text when she told me Rosie was on the way, or when I pinned her to the nursery door and forced her to talk. Hell, she can hardly even look at me on the rare occasions we have to be around each other. Take tonight, for instance. Maddie and Harley are keeping the kids, JoJo included, so we guys can go out. I can guarantee she will hide and avoid me during the time I am there. Same as next weekend when we keep the kids so the ladies can go out. She has become rather crafty at it, too. At first, she would hide in the bathroom when I would stop by. Now she just walks right past me like I'm not even there, or she keeps herself so busy jumping and taking care of any and everything around the house. Walking around with headphones on so that she can't hear me when I call her name. If it weren't so fucking frustrating, I would laugh and applaud her. Maddie still refuses to tell me anything.

'It's her story to tell, Jack. She will tell you when she is ready. You just need to be ready to hear it and comfort her.' Yeah, how can I be prepared for something I have no clue about? Madds never has an answer for that. Just a sad smile and a pat on my back, like that helps.

"Hey, fuck-face. You about ready to head out?" Justin's obnoxious voice calls from my front door. Son-of-a-bitch.

"Who just walks into someone's house like that?" I growl, scrubbing my hand down my face.

"You, you used to do the same thing to me all the fucking time, before Maddie and the twins moved in." Xander chuckles from behind Justin.

"What the hell are you doing here, asshole? Weren't we supposed to meet at your house?" I ask him as I get up from my seat on the couch.

"You didn't answer your phone when I called to tell you Maddie wanted you to pack JoJo some extra clothes. They are going to the park and go out for ice cream. So, we thought we would come by to make sure you haven't drunk yourself into a coma or something." Xan says with a shrug of his shoulder.

I flip him the bird as I walk down the hall to JoJo's room to add some extra clothes to her overnight bag. She is just waking up from a nap when I walk into her room.

"Is it time to go, daddy?" She asks while rubbing the sleep from her eyes. JoJo rarely takes naps, but we had a rough night last night. She has had a few since Harley left us. She will wake up crying looking for me, worried that I have left her too. It breaks my heart that this little girl worries that I will walk away from her like her mom did and like Harley did. I have tried to explain to her that wasn't what Harley had done. She was trying to get away from me. But JoJo doesn't understand it. To her, Harley left the same as her mom.

"Yeah, Little Monster. It's time to go. Are you excited to see the twins and Rosie?" I ask her, pulling her into my arm and snuggling her close. This girl has quickly become my universe.

"Yes!" she exclaims, wiggling out of my arms and grabbing her doll and blanket, ready to leave. I stuff some more clothes in her bag and follow her out the door. Xan and Justin are still standing by the front door when we come back into the living room. After JoJo makes a quick run to the potty, we are heading out.

"We can all go in my truck." Justin offers as we walk down the front steps.

"Sounds good to me, man. Just let me grab this Little Monster's booster seat real fast." I walk over to my truck, grab her seat, and head over to Justin's truck to put it in the back. While I am getting her settled in and buckled up, I hear Xan asking Justin about my house and the progress they have made.

"It will be ready to move in by next month?" Xan sounds genuinely surprised by how fast Justin and his crew worked. Even though he witnessed it himself when they were doing the work on his place. Although, it is a big difference between building a house from the ground up than doing some minor repairs and updates.

"If everything goes as smooth as it has, they should be able to move in by the end of this month. We are down to the final touches now. Painting, cabinets and putting down the hardwood floors." Justin shrugs. "It's looking like we will be done in the next week."

"Damn man. You guys are good," Xan says.

"I have a damn good crew working for me, and this is the only thing we are working on right now. We will start the new subdivision going up in Blackstone in a few weeks."

"That should keep you guys busy for a while," I add to the conversation as we all get into the truck, heading to Xan's and dropping JoJo off before meeting up with Sam.

It doesn't take long to drop JoJo off. Harley was nowhere in sight when we got there. Surprise, surprise. Now we are pulling up to Reapers Axe Tavern. It's new and has a lot of things to do, from arcade games to go-cart racing. There's even axe throwing, pool tables, paintball, and anything else you could think of. The plus side, it's for adults, so there is also alcohol. Although I would not suggest drinking while throwing axes, that could cause some serious injuries. Ten out of ten doctors would probably not recommend it. The plan is to hit the axe throwing before the drinking commences, then on to the safer activities and drink without having to worry about getting your arm chopped off. This place is like a man-child's Chucky Cheese. It is going to be a fun night. Unfortunately, one of us has to stay sober to drive home, and yours truly drew the short stick on that front. Just a minor bump in the road, but tonight will be fun either way. Sam ended up meeting us here since he has something to do in the morning and has to skip out early. But now that we are all here, we are ready for some fun.

We had an awesome time. Of course, everything turned into a competition. How could it not with the four grown-ass men that have the mentality of teenagers when it comes to playing games? Sam won every round of axe throwing, I won in go-cart racing because I have mad driving skills, and Xan kicked our asses in almost every round of pool. I swear the drunker he got, the better he played. Justin beat us in almost every arcade game there was, except for the shooting games, Sam won those. We were like overgrown kids the whole night. It was a much-needed escape from everything going on. The thought of taking Harley there crossed my mind on more than one occasion during the night. It was a fight to keep her out of my thoughts, much like it is every other day. She seems to be on my mind more than not these days. It is getting harder to not force her to open up to me. *Time.* She needs time. Fuck time. I have been waiting long enough. The first chance I get to corner her, I'm taking it. She will tell me what is going on. Tell me what the fuck I did so wrong that made her leave me, leave us. I can't fix things if she isn't willing to talk to me about them. We would be perfect together. I know she felt it too, but she keeps hiding from me. It was not just about the sex as mind-blowing as it was. We mesh perfectly in every way. From raising JoJo, to everyday things like what to watch after a long day, making dinner together, or just sitting down and enjoying a beer together. Forcing her to talk will have to wait until tomorrow since JoJo is staying the night over there. It will give me some time to form a plan that I hope will work.

I WAKE UP BRIGHT AND EARLY TO PUT MY PLAN INTO motion. Only to find out it won't happen today. She won't be there when I pick up JoJo. She has things to do, according to Maddie. No matter, she won't be able to avoid me at their wedding, seeing as she is the Maid of Honor, and I am the Best Man. I will be the one to walk her down the aisle. We will have to dance together, take pictures together, and eat at the same table. I will do everything in my power to work her up, get her hot and bothered, and then hold out on her, not giving her what she needs until she tells me what the fuck is going on. It is perfect. Is it wrong to purposely arouse her, during a wedding with all of our friends and family around, to use her needs against her for answers? To get my way, yes, yes, it is. Will I be doing that without a single regret? Fuck yes, I will and will enjoy every second of it. Pulling up at Xan's I push my devious plan to the back of my mind, hop out of my truck, and head inside to get my little girl. We have some shopping to do. She is picking out a big girl bedroom suite today for her new room, and we will need to pick out some for the spare rooms as well.

"Hey, man. She is just finishing up breakfast. Come on in." Xander says as he steps aside for me to walk in.

"Was she good for y'all?" I ask Maddie as I pull her into a hug.

"You know she is always a perfect little angel," Maddie informs me. I hear JoJo's squeal of excitement and her little feet pounding across the hardwood floors before I see her. Seth is chasing her into the living room with his hands held out like he is going to tickle her.

"Daddy, Daddy, save me." She squeals, laughing as she launches herself into my arms.

"Sup, Jack." Seth gives me a chin nod, like he is a grown-ass man. "I'll catch you next time, Little Monster." He tells JoJo with a smile.

"My princess," JoJo tells him, sticking her tongue out, causing us all to laugh.

"Why were you chasing this sweet princess?" Maddie asks Seth as she coos at JoJo.

"I told her if she stole my cookie when I went to the bathroom, I would tickle her until she peed her pants. When I came back, she had taken a big bite." He shrugs his shoulder and JoJo sticks her tongue out again.

"That wasn't very nice, Little Monster. Why would you take a bite of his cookie?" I ask, looking down at her.

"It was so good, daddy." She tells me, making her eyes go wide like I should already know how good the cookie was. It takes everything in me not to laugh.

"It's fine, really. I knew she was going to steal a bite; it was the last cookie. That's why I left it there and told her I would tickle her if she did." Seth says before he heads up the stairs. "By Little Monster." He calls over his shoulder before he disappears around the corner.

"Thank you for keeping her Madds. We will see you guys later; we need to go buy some furniture for the new house." I say, grabbing JoJo's bag off the couch.

"Any time, I love having her here," Maddie tells me before placing a kiss on JoJo's cheek and hugging me.

"See y'all later, man," Xan calls as we walk down the steps heading to my truck.

"Later man."

It doesn't take JoJo long to pick out a new bedroom suite. She, of course, went with a canopy bed, fit for a princess. We went with the wood frame, so it was sturdier and would last longer. Hopefully, because this shit sure isn't cheap. I stuck with a farmhouse theme for the spare room, keeping it simple since it will rarely be used. The room will only have a bed and a chest of drawers. I plan to keep my bed just as it is. No need to get a new one, when the one I have is perfect. The iron rails of the headboard give me the perfect place to tie Harley's hands when we want to play and play, we will when I bring her back home. Tying her up and spanking that tight little ass of her is high on my list of things to do after these long months of torture. Being able to see her but not touch her, not have her in my arms, or under me where she belongs. Yeah, I would say she has more than earned a good ass tanning by my hands and how I am looking forward to seeing my handprint on that ass once again. I am hard as steel just thinkin' about it, thinking about all the fun we have had together, and all the fun we will have again. Because she will be mine. No way in hell I will let her go. She belongs with me. I just have to make her see it as well. She will, she will see how much I love her. How well I can take care of her. She knows there isn't another man that can work her body like I can. No other man can make her scream their name late into the night like I can. How do I know this? I may have overheard her talking to Maddie one night. Definitely not one of my finer moments, lurking around a corner, eavesdropping on their personal conversation, but I needed answers that neither of them are willing to give. The answers I got, might not be the ones I was looking for, but I didn't mind hearing them. Hearing their conversation helped me to come up with the plan to get Harley to talk. Now it's just a waiting game to put my plan into motion.

Chapter 20

HARLEY

It is time to party; well party might be a strong word for what we have planned. Maddie does not want to go out on the town and get wild. She's still breastfeeding Rosie and says she is too old for all that. I rolled my eyes so hard I was sure they would be stuck looking at the back of my skull for the rest of my life. The rest of us would love nothing more than to get shit-faced and dance the night away. But since this night is all for Maddie, we will do no such thing. Instead, we have rented a suite at a big hotel in Beckinsdale; they have a spa that we have purchased the full works for all of us. Being pampered all day in the spa and then chilling in the pool after. That's the plan, plus we still have some wine and play some games in our hotel suite. Becky is bringing her mom's Roomba, the little vacuum that' moves around on its own, so I can attach a suction cup dildo to it and some of those pool rings so we can play ring toss. For no other reason than it's going to be funny as hell trying to get a ring around the cock that is zooming around on top of a robotic vacuum. We also got some other naughty bachelorette party games. Like pin the penis on the hunk, boob dodge ball, they are actual boob shaped stress balls... nipples and all. I will adorn our drinks with penis straws, and virgin drinks for Madds since she is not drinking. Penis-shaped cookies, and cupcakes decorated with penises. Let's just say there will be tons of dicks at this little shindig, just not attached to the male specimen. Which is as equally refreshing as it is depressing.

To say I have been in a funk for the last, what, three months, or has it been four? Hell, I can't remember now. Since I left Jack's, funk would be an understatement. I have not gone this long without being railed since I was seventeen and lost my V-card. I have gone out a few times with the intentions o' finding someone, especially after Jack and Justin went out drinking one night when JoJo stayed over with Sammie. I know that is what his intentions were, I'm sure of it. So, why am I sitting around missing him, not getting my itched scratched when I could be? I couldn't go through with it though, not even when D called me up asking if I wanted to get a drink. He was always a fun time, but he can't compare to Jack. He has truly ruined me for all men, just like he said he would do. It's all my fault, I know it is. I have been too chicken-shit to talk to him, to tell him about my fears and why I ran. It breaks my heart that he still feels like it was something he had done wrong. No matter how many times

I tell him otherwise, he keeps thinking the worst of himself. I know all about that, though. Our childhoods are way too similar, being abandoned by the people who should have loved us unconditionally, really fucked both of us up. Even when you think you are over the trauma, that you have outgrown it, it rears its ugly head, bringing out all your insecurities and doubts. It always finds a way to creep back in, to convince you that you are worthless, unlovable, and dispensable. It's a burden that was handed to us at an early age that will follow us around for the rest of our lives like a foul smell. Does that mean that we can ever overcome it? No, it just means when something gets us down, makes us feel unwanted, we remind ourselves how we were discarded like trash before, so why would now be any different? Then we have to work that much harder to remind ourselves we deserve better than that. To know I am the reason Jack is experiencing those feelings of uncertainty guts me.

"Hey girly, what's the matter?" Maddie asks me as she sits down beside me on the couch, wrapping me in a one-armed hug. Rosie snuggled safely in the other, snoozing away. I had not realized just how long I had been sitting here staring at the wall until she pulled me from my thoughts.

"Just thinking," I tell her with a weak smile on my face. I don't have to elaborate on what I was thinking about. She already knows. After all, she is my best friend, she always knows what is bothering me. Well, almost always. I guess I kept a big secret from her for a long time, but not anymore. She knows it all now.

"You need to talk to him, Harley. You can't fix things if you don't." She says softly, rubbing my back.

"I know, I will... just after your wedding. I don't want to cause any drama." I tell her which earns me the stink-eye.

"How would you cause drama by talking to Jack?" she asks.

"I don't know. If we are talking, we could end up fighting. If we aren't talking, then we can't fight." I tell her. She just stares at me for a moment. A look of contemplation appears on her face. I can almost see the gears spinning in that pretty little head of hers.

"You won't fight." She says with all the confidence in the world.

"How..." she cuts me off before I can finish my question.

"You won't fight because that man loves you. All he wants is to love you, be with you, and take care of you. No, you won't fight. I'd be more worried that he would try to fuck your brains out on the dance floor for everyone to see." She snickers.

"Madeline Grace." I gasp. I can't believe she said that. Since she found out she was pregnant, I haven't heard a cussword leave her mouth. She always substitutes them now. Fudge, that's her go-to lately.

"What? You know it's true." She says, full-on laughing now.

"Shush, you're going to wake Rosie," I tell her, covering her mouth with my hand, trying not to laugh myself. "True or not. I still think it's best to wait." She gives me a sad smile.

We sit there for a few moments, not saying a word until it is time to head out. We left the kids with Xan for now. Jack and

JoJo will be there later to keep them company. We are meeting Becky and Hope at the hotel. It's time for fun. No more depressing thoughts for the rest of the day. Becky and Hope both have things to do tomorrow and wanted to have their own cars. Maddie and I are going back to the same place, so it made more sense for us to drive up together. This hotel is absolutely gorgeous. It kind of looks like a modern-day castle. It is huge, surrounded by lush green grass, perfectly trimmed hedges, and beautiful mature trees. Everything is clean and all the staff seem friendly. It didn't take us long to check-in, and the nice bellboy took all of our bags up to the room. How funny would it have been if the bag with the variety of dicks popped open in his hands? He would have been scarred for life and I, for one, would have found it hilarious.

We got the full spa treatment. Body scrubs, body wraps, massages, facials, eye, lip, hand, scalp, and hair treatments. We got waxed, plucked, and even treated ourselves to mani-pedis. After we were done with our spa treatments, we spent significantly more time than we needed to in the steam room. By the time we made it to our room for the evening, we were all more relaxed than we have ever been. When I broke out the games, all the girls hoot and hollered. We had a blast. If you would have told me before last night that it could be that a lot of fun partying sober, I would have laughed in your face. But I guess when you are with the right people, you can make anything fun. I thought Maddie would piss herself laughing when the Roomba started scooting around the room with a twelve-inch dildo on top of it. That thing was harder to ring than I anticipated it to be. Not one of us managed to pin the penis on the hunk, well not in the proper spot, anyway. Sometimes being blindfolded seriously has its disadvantages. The cookies and cupcakes were an enormous hit. We even saved some for the guys. I, for one, cannot wait to see their faces when we give those to them. All in all, it was a fabulous night out with the girls. We should do it more often.

"I don't know if I can do this." I squeak out, causing Maddie to double over in laughter.

"Isn't that supposed to be my line today?" She barely gets out between laughing and trying to catch her breath.

"Suck a dick Madds. I am hyperventilating over here and you are laughing. What kind of friend are you?" I huff out as I return to pacing the room that we are currently getting ready in.

"Calm down, Sugarplum. It's going to be fine." Becky says cheerfully.

"It's not like you're the one getting hitched." Hope points out, unhelpfully.

"Fuck you, fuck all three of you so very much," I say, glaring at my now ex-friends. Am I being a big baby? Possible. Should I calm down, suck it up, force a smile on my face and enjoy my best friend's wedding? Most definitely.

"We can trade spots. Jack can walk me, and Justin can walk

you." Becky offers, while Hope's eyes go wide, and she shakes her head no like that takes the suggestion away. The scowl I throw Becky's way is accompanied by a growl that has her holding her hand up and backing away.

"I wasn't trying to steal your best friend's spot. Just offering to walk with the man you don't want to walk with." Becky tries to defend herself.

"Not helping. Shut up." Hope hisses.

"What? She's too scared to face him, and he has to walk one of us. I was just trying to help." Becky explains.

Would it be poor etiquette to strangle one friend on another friend's wedding day? Probably so. Maybe I should refrain from doing that. I clench my hand on my hips. Trying to steady my rapid breathing. It does nothing to help. *I think I am having a heart attack. That's what this is. I'm going to drop dead here and now.*

"Harley, breath. Calm down. Look at me, I thought you said you could do this?" Maddie is now holding me by my shoulders, looking concerned. At least she's not laughing anymore.

"I thought I could," I whisper, fighting back tears. She wraps me in a tight hug. I needed that. I can feel myself slowly start to relax, my breathing becoming more even, and my eyes are no longer burning.

"Thank you," I say, hugging her back.

"What are friends for? Now, do you want to talk about it? Maybe apologize to Becky for growling at her like you're not housebroken." Becky and Hope snort out a laugh that has a smile tugging at my lips.

"Sorry, he's mine. You're not allowed to touch." I say, playfully.

"And here I was thinking you were upset that I was trying to take your maid of honor spot." Becky jokes, her eyes wide like she is shocked.

"Phish..." I blow air past my lips like the thought of her taking my spot in Maddie's life wouldn't be a big deal. It would devastate me for sure, but another woman on Jack's arm, I don't think I could survive that. "I think I am good now. Sorry for the freak out guys." I say, shaking out my limbs and preparing myself to face Jack. *'I can do this.'* Deep breath. *'I can do this.'* If I just keep repeating it to myself, maybe it will come true.

A knock at the door has all of our heads snapping up. "It's time girls, are you ready?" Calls Dan's voice from the other side of the door. A huge smile forms on Maddie's face. I am so happy for my best friend. She deserves this day after all the hell she has been through, and I am determined not to let my scared little ass ruin it for her. Pulling my shoulder back and forcing a smile on my face, I nod my head, letting her know I am okay and ready to get this show on the road.

"Ready Daddy," Maddie calls back, and we all make our way out the door. Dan holds his arm out to Maddie as we start to walk down the long hallway leading to the double doors, we will be walking through in just a few moments.

"You look beautiful, baby girl," Dan whispers as tears streak down his face.

"Don't cry Daddy, you'll make me cry, then all the work we put into making my face look this good goes down the drain." Dan chuckles at his daughter. When we reach the end of the hall, I come to a complete stop. I can hear Jack's deep laugh and mumbled words. I don't know if I can turn the corner. My feet are frozen in place. I don't have much of a choice when one of my evil friends pushes me forward.

'Maybe strangulation isn't completely off of the table for today after all.' My heart leaps into my throat when my eyes land on Jack, drinking him in from head to toe. Fucking hell, he looks delicious in a tux. Why does he have to look so damn good? All of my lady bits perk up at the sight of him. My mouth waters and I am almost positive both of my ovaries just exploded, or maybe I have become pregnant just from the heated look he just threw my way. I can feel tingles on every inch of my body as his lust-filled eyes take me in. There is no way in hell I am surviving this night without becoming a puddle of aching need at his feet. I am praying for the floor to swallow me up now. My heart skips at least ten beats when he steps up to me and circles around me, looking me up and down. But when he stops behind me, standing so close that his front is firmly pressed into my back. His hands land on my hip, holding me in place, and he leans down so his lips graze my ear as he speaks. All of a sudden, I forget how to breathe.

"Damn Princess, you are so fucking beautiful, hell, breathtakingly beautiful. You look better than every man's best wet dream." He growls in my ear and my legs turn to jello on the spot. The only thing holding me up is his firm grip on my hips. His chuckle vibrates my back and forces me out of the spell he put me under. I step out of his hold, taking a deep breath.

"Meh, you clean up okay, I guess," I say, trying to sound unaffected. He's not buying it. He throws his head back, laughing. Stupid men and their stupid hotness.

Chapter 21

JACK

HARLEY IS A VISION IN HER MAID OF HONOR'S DRESS. Hell, she is a sight to be seen, no matter what she is wearing. My eyes trail the length of her body when she walked in. My cock decided right then that it was the perfect time to come to life. Like everyone here needs to witness him straining to be free, to get what she has deprived him of for too long. I swagger over to her, circling her a few times, drinking in every inch of her perfect body wrapped in her form-fitting dress. Taking note of the convenient slit in the front that almost reaches her hip. If I wasn't sure before I stepped into her that my plan will work, I am positive it will now. I press myself against her back, holding her hip so she can't move away, and lean down to whisper in her ear.

"Damn Princess, you are so fucking beautiful, hell, breathtakingly beautiful. You look better than every man's best wet dream." What was supposed to be a whisper comes out more of a growl, and her breath catches in her throat, her knees go weak. I have to tighten my hold on her hips to keep her from falling to the ground. She seems to regain control of herself when I chuckle at Justin, who is fake fanning himself across the room. Asshole.

"Meh, you clean up okay, I guess." Harley throws back at me, trying and failing to act like I don't phase her. I throw my head back, laughing. This is going to be fun and riling her up is going to be way too easy.

I would love to say that the wedding was beautiful, that Maddie and Xander's vows brought a tear to my eyes and warmed my heart. But I would be lying. I am sure it was, and their vows possibly would have warmed my heart, had I been able to focus on anything other than the beauty standing across from me. The entire walk down the aisle, all I could envision was our wedding day. Standing across from her, all I can think about is what I would say to her when the Preacher asks for us to recite our vows. Saying I do and me dipping her back, taking her lips with mine for the first time as husband and wife. Would her face light up with happiness? Would she have tears in her eyes from being filled with so much joy it physically hurts? Is she thinking the same things I am? Her eyes haven't left mine this whole time, so I know her focus is solely on me. Much like mine are on her. Would she regret marrying me? Years down the road, would she look back on the day asking herself what the fuck she was thinking, giving herself to someone like me?

Would I be her biggest mistake or part of her happiest moments? Are these the kind of thoughts everyone has at weddings? The worries that plague everyone's minds, or is it just me? The smile she gives me fills me with hope as she takes my arm again for me to lead her back down the aisle. One more step closer to having my girl back.

After pictures, food, and speeches, everyone moved to the dance floor. We all stood to the side watching as Xander twirled Maddie across the dance floor for their first dance, as well as Dan and Maddie for the father-daughter dance. I look around, trying to spot Harley as everybody grabs a dance partner and heads out onto the floor. For a moment I think she has left, until I spot her dancing with Pops, laughing at something he had said. I give them a few moments before I cut in, enjoying the happiness that is visible on her face. It feels like it has been a lifetime since the last time I saw a real smile grace that beautiful face, and I make a vow right then and there to make sure to always try my hardest to keep that smile in place. I know I will make mistakes. Fuck things up royally if I know me, which I do. But I also know I would give my life to keep her and JoJo happy. Speaking of JoJo, I take another look around and spot her, forcing Seth to dance. That kid, she is a hand full, but one I would not trade for the world. She has brought more joy into my life than I thought possible. Now that I know she is good, I set my sights back on Harley. Pushing my way through the dancing bodies, I walk up beside them and clear my throat.

"Can I cut in?" I ask, not taking my eyes off of her.

"If that's all right with you," Harley says to Pops with a sweet as sugar smile on her face. He nods, places a kiss on her cheek, and steps back. Before he can respond, Harley is talking again.

"You two have a nice dance now." She says, then starts past me. Pops roars with laughter, shaking his head and walking away. I grunt, wrap my arm around Harley's waist, and drag her back into my arms.

"I don't think so. You're being a bad girl, Princess. Do I need to spank you here in front of everybody?" She shivers in my arm as a small moan escapes her lips.

"Let's not do this here Jack, I'd rather not make a scene." She tells me even as she lets her head fall back onto my shoulder. I sway us side to side, refusing to let her go now that she is back in my arms.

"One dance baby. Please, give me that." I plead with her. My heart plummets to the floor beneath my feet when she pulls out of my arms. I'm almost certain I've lost her for good until she turns around and wraps her arms around my neck. We don't speak, we just dance as I hum to the music. Swinging us around the dance floor. Finally, feeling whole again.

Three songs. That's what she gives me before she is pulling away again. Taking my heart right along with her. It takes far longer than I would like to admit before I come to my senses and hunt her down. No way is she just walking away from us like that again. I deserve answers, if nothing else. I know she feels at least something for me. She leaves me high and dry, and

I am sick and tired of it. I spot her dipping into a room off the side, and I follow her in. Taking a quick look around, I notice it is some type of conference room. There's an enormous table in the center of the room with chairs all around it. The best part is there is no one else around, just the two of us.

"Stop running from me, Shadow. We need to talk about this. Tell me what is going on, please. You are killing me here." She apparently didn't hear me walk in because she jumps at the sound of my voice.

"Not now Jack. I promise, after the wedding is over, we will talk. I just don't want to mess up Maddie and Xander's day." She sits down on the edge of the table, looking back down at her feet. Moving in front of her, I place my finger under her chin, forcing her eyes back up to mine.

"No, I am done waiting. I have waited four months. We are talking about this now. Look around, Shadow. There is no one in her but you and me. No one else to hear your secrets." I tell her, moving in closer, I wedge my knee between her thighs, forcing the split in her dress to fall open, revealing her long tan leg to me. I drag my palm up her thigh, watching goose flesh appear. My mouth is against her neck, I murmur.

"If you don't want to freely give me your secrets, I will be forced to drag them out of you. One orgasm at a time, Princess." I trail kisses along her neck, across her jaw until my lips are on hers and I am kissing her with all the passion and lust that has been building in me all night. Hell, for the past four months. She moans into the kiss, and I take full advantage, sweeping my tongue into her mouth, massaging her tongue with mine. She kisses me back with as much force as I am giving her, matching me, not relenting, not backing down. When my hand slips up between her legs, I groan at the feeling of her bare flesh against my hand. Warm and soaking wet for me.

"God damn, My Little Shadow, you are a naughty little thing, aren't you? What were you thinking, prancing around all night with no panties on?" She gasps out a moan when I push a finger into her tight little cunt.

"Fuck, so good." She groans, riding my hand. I lean my body in closer, stopping her movements and still mine.

"Answer me, baby," I demand.

"I was thinking it would be fewer clothes for you to remove later if you took me home." She whimpers, trying to grind her hip down, but I won't let her move.

"You want to go home with me? You tell me what had you running away from me for four months." I add another finger and pump them in and out of her. Driving her needs higher and higher before stopping again.

"Talk, Harley, or I stop and go back to the wedding," I growl out.

"Fuck, okay, okay. I'll tell you, but you have to remove your fingers. No way I can talk about this with your fingers inside me." I slowly remove my fingers and take a step back, giving her some space. She gives me a heated look and a small whimper when I moan as her flavors burst on my tongue when I lick my fingers clean.

"I got married right out of high school." She says, the word coming out so fast they jumble together.

"You still married?" I ask with a raised brow. It would certainly put a damper on my plans, but wouldn't stop me from being with her, seeing as they are not still together.

"Would you still want me if I was?" she asks me, tilting her head to the side, watching for any signs of a lie from me. She won't find one.

"Fuck yeah, and I'd pay for the divorce," I tell her.

"Interesting." She says. I shrug and she continues. "No, I'm not still married. He actually filed for divorce after I had two miscarriages and he got his secretary pregnant."

"Fucking dickhead." I grunt.

"I've called him that a few times, amongst other things. Anyway, the divorce isn't important. We were never in love, we only got married because I found out I was pregnant. His parents would not approve if we had a baby out of wedlock." She rolls her eyes. "The issue is with me. After the first miscarriage, I got an infection. It left behind scar tissue, and then I got pregnant again, well before my body was ready because that's what he wanted. I lost it too." I sit in a chair beside her and pull her into my arms, holding her tight against me.

"I'm so sorry, baby. I hate that you had to go through that." I tell her, not sure what else I can say. I just know she needs some comfort at the moment, so I sit here in silence, just holding her until she is ready to tell me the rest of her story.

I don't know how long we sit here before she gathers her

thoughts and looks up at me with tears in her eyes. I almost tell her she doesn't have to tell me more. We can just go back to the wedding, leave, and do this later. Anything to wipe that devastating look off of her face. But when I open my mouth, she covers it with her hand, shaking her head as a tear slides down her cheek. I swipe it away with my thumb.

"The doctor did surgery to remove the scar tissue but said that they can't guarantee that I would carry full term if I was to get pregnant again. When you thought I was asleep, you said you wanted me to be the mother of your children. I may never be able to give that. I got scared and left. I'm sorry I hurt you and JoJo. I just didn't know how to face it. How to tell you, I couldn't give you what you want." More tears fall from her eyes, and I swear my heart bleeds for her.

"Please don't cry, baby. You don't know what seeing your tears does to me. It feels like you are ripping my heart from my chest with every single one that falls." I tell her truthfully, as I clean the tears from her cheek.

"Could you... would you still want me even if I couldn't give you kids?" She asks, looking back down into her lap.

"Harley, look at me." Her eyes slowly move back up to mine. "I would still want to spend the rest of my life loving you, whether you give me kids or not. Zero kids or ten kids makes no difference. All I need is you. You and JoJo. I would be the happiest man alive. Besides, the fun part is trying to make the babies right." I tell her, wagging my brows, trying to lighten the mood some. It does the trick. She laughs, swatting at my chest before laying her head on my shoulder.

"Are you sure?" She asks a few moments later.

"You couldn't beat me away with a stick, Princess. You're mine, forever. Are you ready to go home? JoJo is staying the night with the twins at Maddie's parents. We will have the house to ourselves."

"Yeah, let's go home. Oh, and Jack." She says as we stand to head to the door. I stop looking down at her. "I love you." She tells me with a huge smile on her face. All thoughts of going home have officially left. I back her up to the table.

"Say it again," I tell her. Cupping my face in her palms, she gives to my demand.

"I love you, Jack. I love you so fucking much." My lips are on hers in an instance. By the time we break away from the kiss, we are both panting.

"I love you too, My Little Shadow, more than you know," I tell her before kissing her again.

Our kiss goes from gentle and loving to hot and needy. Before I can again suggest that we get out of here, she is undoing my pants and setting the monster free from the cage he has been fighting all night. Wrapping her hand around my length, she strokes from root to tip, and I'm surprised I don't cum on the spot. It has been too long, and I need her to cum first. Pulling her hand from around me, I drop to my knees in front of her, push her dress up past her hips, throw one of her legs over my shoulder, and feast on her delectable cunt. Fuck, I have missed this woman. Using my thumbs, I spread her slick lips, dragging the flat of my tongue through her folds. Her flavor dancing on my tongue causes a possessive growl to rumble through my chest. Harley whimpers, tangling her fingers into my hair and grinding her pussy against my face. I double down on my efforts. Slipping one, then two fingers inside her dripping center, I pump them in time with the flicks and licks of my tongue on her clit. Sucking her clit into my mouth, I bite down hard enough to make her hips buck against my face. She lets out a cry of pleasure and I massage my fingers over her g-spot. Her orgasm crashes through her, flooding my mouth. I drink down every last drop, like a man who has been lost in a desert for years. I can't get enough of this woman. I catch her when her legs give out beneath her. Getting to my feet, I lay her across the table, trailing my hands up her smooth thighs. I can't wait any longer. I have to be balls deep inside her wet heat.

Lining up with her entrance, I slowly push in up to the hilt. Groaning as her walls squeeze the shit out of me. I plow in and out of her with such force; I have to hold her hips to keep her from moving up the table. I thrust until we are both falling over the edge, calling out each other's names. Pulling out of her, I help her to her feet. Holding her close to me. More than ready to get out of here, take her home, and take my time loving every inch of her.

"You ready to get out of here, Princess?" I ask her, placing a kiss on the top of her head.

"We didn't use a condom, Jack." She states, her face paling before my eyes.

"Yeah, we haven't used one in a while. I haven't been with anyone since you, Harley. It's okay."

"You don't understand. I quit taking my birth control a few months back. There is a chance I could end up pregnant. I don't think I can handle it right now. What if I lose the baby? It would kill me." She is freaking out now.

"Hey, calm down, baby. Look, I know you are scared, rightfully so, but you will be fine. If we get pregnant and lose the baby, I will be by your side the entire time. You will never have to go through anything alone again. We will mourn together, cry together, heal together. Always together, Princess."

"Promise?" She asks, looking up at me with hope shining in her eyes. I hold up my pinky finger like I do with JoJo and wrap it around Harley's.

"Pinky promise, Princess. I swear to you, I will be by your side through everything life throws our way 'til the day I die." She gives me a quick peck on the cheek before we walk out hand in hand to head home. Life can't get better than this.

Epilogue

JACK

This last month has been one of the best months of my life. Harley has moved back in with us, and this time into my room instead of the spare room. We are in the new house now and since Harley no longer needed the trailer; we sold it. It has been moved and now we are trying to decide what to do with the extra space in the yard. JoJo and Harley have never been closer. It's like they are connected at the hip, and I wouldn't change it. They do everything together. They go shopping, they go to the nail salon, even though I think JoJo is too young for it. Although Harley only lets her get her nails painted light colors and never lets her get fake nails. They are like two peas in a pod. JoJo is doing fantastic in Pre-k, and she loves her teacher. Harley and I may have cried the first day we dropped her off, but not JoJo. She ran off and started making new friends. It was like we were not even there at all. She started a little late. All the other kids started in August, but JoJo's birthday is September eighteenth, so I refused to let her start before then. Thankfully, the school didn't mind working with us, given the fact that JoJo was still adjusting to living with me. They didn't want to rush her any more than I did. Today we kept her out. She is going down to the courthouse with us. Harley and I are getting married, and Harley is adopting JoJo. Have I told you my life is perfect?

Pulling up outside of the courthouse, I hop out of my truck and help JoJo down from the back seat. Spotting Xan standing up on the stairs, I grab JoJo's hand and head over to him.

"Hey man, they get here yet?" I ask him. Harley and Madds are meeting us here. Maddie was adamant that Harley needed a dress. She could care less either way but went along with it.

"Called just a few minutes ago, they should pull up any second now. Hey, sweetheart. You ready for today?" Xan asks JoJo.

"Yes sir, I get a new mommy." She beams at him. For the last two weeks, she has been looking forward to today. She asked Harley to adopt her when we get married and Harley was more than happy to do so. I was prepared to plan a big wedding, but Harley refused. Said she didn't need a big to do. Just us and a few friends were all she needed. I keep feeling like I am letting her down in some way, but she wouldn't hear anything about a wedding. I think some of it has to do with the fact that she had done it before and it didn't work out, so she wants to do it differently this time around. As long as My Little Shadow and Little Monster are happy, I am happy. It's not long before Harley and Maddie have pulled up, as well as Becky, Justin, Sam, Hope, Dan, Tracy, and Pops. Looks like it's time to get this show on the road. I quickly make my way over to Harley's door, helping her out.

"You ready to become Mrs. Williams?" I ask, pulling her into my arms for a kiss.

"More than ready." She tells me, nipping at my bottom lip.

"You sure you are ready to adopt JoJo? I don't want you to feel pressured. You can wait if you need to." I tell her, hoping she doesn't take it the wrong way. I want nothing more, but don't want her to say yes just because she thinks that's what I want.

"I am more sure about being her mom than I am about being your wife. I just kinda got stuck with you. I am choosing JoJo." She teases me with a wink before walking inside holding our daughter's hand. Our daughter. That has a nice ring to it. Damn, I am one lucky son-of-a-bitch.

HARLEY

It is Christmas time again. It seems like it was just yesterday that Maddie and Xander were announcing their pregnancy to everyone on Christmas morning. It's been a year though. A whole year and so much has happened. Jack found out he has a daughter. We have a daughter. She is officially mine now as well. We got married, and I adopted JoJo. Now I get to tell them that we are having a baby. Am I still scared shitless? Fuck yes, I am. But do I trust Jack will be by my side every step of the way, no matter the outcome? Yes, one hundred percent, yes. He has more than proven he is in this until the very end. I am so thankful Maddie met Xander, because not only did it bring joy into their lives, but it brought Jack back into mine. How we were in this small town together for years and never ran into each other, I will never know. So, here's the plan, so I don't freak out and not announce it to everyone else before I tell Jack. I am telling Jack right along with all of our friends and family when we exchange gifts later at Maddie and Xander's house. I hid the gifts for Jack and JoJo at the back of their tree the other day when we dropped off all the presents. Which, by the way, was difficult. Why do men think they have to carry everything, like women are fragile or some shit? Maddie and Xander are under strict instructions to give them the gifts at the same time. I really hope he doesn't mind finding out this way.

After JoJo opened all the gifts Santa had brought her, along with the ones from us, we had breakfast and now we are headed to open gifts with the family. JoJo is bouncing in her seat with excitement at the thought of more gifts and getting to play with the kids. I am on pins and needles, praying Jack doesn't get upset that I didn't tell him before announcing it to everyone. No one knows right now besides me and my OBGYN.

I had to know it wasn't a false pregnancy, and that everything looked okay before I said anything.

"You alright Shadow?" Jack questions as we pull up at Maddie and Xander's. "I know you weren't feeling well the other day. We can go home if you need to. I'm sure they won't mind if we miss this year if you aren't feeling better yet." Why does this man pay so damn much attention to me? It's like he doesn't miss a thing.

"I feel fine, I promise. You worry too much." I tell him with a big smile before I kiss his cheek and hop out of the truck. I help JoJo get out and we all walk in together as a family, holding hands. Just think, next year it will be four of us.

"Hey," Maddie says with a big smile as she opens the door. "Everyone's here now." She calls over her shoulder as we walk in. I guess we are the last to show up. Not surprisingly, JoJo changed dresses five times before she settled on the one I had picked out for her to start with. She is such a little diva. Jack swears she is just like me. I only smacked him once for that. Because he's not wrong, but damnit, did he have to point it out?

It's not long before everyone has found a place to sit in the living room. Xan and Pops are passing out gifts to kids first, then the adults. As I requested, they save my gifts for last. Fuck, I am nervous. I'm not so sure now that this was the best plan.

"These are from Harley. You both have to open them at the same time." Xander explains to Jack and JoJo as he hands them the gifts. I guess I can't go back now. I watch with bated breaths as they both open the boxes, pulling out matching shirts. Jacks says Daddy of Two. JoJo's says Best Big Sister. Jack stares at the shirt, not talking.

"Mommy, what does it say? JoJo asks me, pulling my gaze down to her.

"It says Best Big Sister," I tell her.

"We..." Jack has to clear his throat before he tries to speak again. "We are having a baby?" He finally gets around the lump in his throat. He has tears in his eyes, and I am still not sure if this was the best way to tell him. The room is almost deathly silent, like they are scared of making a sound. Except for JoJo, who is dancing around.

"I'm gonna be big sister, I'm gonna be a big sister." She sings as she twirls around with her shirt hugged to her.

"I shouldn't have told you like this. I'm sorry. I should have done this at home. I knew better." I ramble. Jack pulls me into his lap, crushing his mouth down on mine, effectively cutting off my apology.

"Shadow, it's perfect. Stop. Are we having a baby?" He asks again, like he still doesn't believe it.

"We are. Are you happy?" I ask him, laying my head on his shoulder.

"The happiest man in the world. Thank you for the best gift a man could ever ask for. I love you, My Little Shadow."

"I love you too." Congratulations ring out through the house and JoJo plops down in our lap.

"I'm gonna be the best big sister." She says, hugging us both tight. It can't get any better than this. I have the love of my life, an amazing daughter, and a baby I thought I would never be able to have on the way. I don't know what I did to deserve this life I have been given, but I thank my lucky stars Jack refused to give up on me even when I had given up on myself. He wanted all or nothing. And now we will have it all.

THE END

OTHER BOOKS BY TILYA

<u>Safe In Love Series</u>
Saving His Angel
All or Nothing
Forever Hers
Everything I need

<u>Shadow Dragons MC</u>
Redeeming Axel

WHERE YOU CAN FIND ME

Facebook author page: Author Tilya Eloff
Facebook author page: Tilya's Tantalizing Readers
Instagram author Page: authortilyaeloff
Twitter author page: AuthorTilya
TikTok author page: authortilyaeloff
Follow me on Amazon
Sign up for my <u>Newsletter</u>
Or check out my Website

ACKNOWLEDGMENTS

Thank you, to my husband, and kids, for not only believing in me but for being patient with me, as I spent so much time in front of my laptop and was sometimes late getting dinner prepared because I was so lost in my writing.

Thank you, to my *AMAZING* PA Tammy Carney, for not only taking me on as a new author and doing an outstanding job but for also becoming an amazing new friend.

Thank you, to my *AMAZING* editor Darcie Fisher, for not only taking me on and working endlessly to help improve my stories but for being such an amazing friend.

I am so blessed to be surrounded by such an elite group of people. To anyone who took the time out to read my book, thank you so much. It means everything to me, that you would take a chance on a brand-new author.

ABOUT AUTHOR

Tilya Eloff was born and raised in a small town in Alabama. A wife, and mom of five, who loves getting lost in a great book, at the end of a busy day. She fell in love with reading, after being diagnosed with Charcot-Marie-Tooth disorder, and could no longer work. She needed something to fill her days while her kids were at school. Recently, she has felt called to writing. Now she considers herself to be an Indie author and just wants to make a living doing what she loves.

NOTE FROM THE AUTHOR

Thank you for taking a chance on me and reading my book. I know not every story is for everyone, and I am truly grateful you took the time out to read mine. I'd appreciate it if you would take the time to leave a review. As an indie author, reviews are really important. Again, thank you so much for taking a chance on me, and reading Saving His Angel. I have two more books planned for this small-town series of interconnected standalone's and can't wait to get started on them. I hope you all have a blessed day, full of love and happiness.

Made in the USA
Columbia, SC
23 February 2024